EX LIBRIS

VINTAGE **CLASSICS**

# J. G. BALLARD

J. G. Ballard was born in 1930 in Shanghai, China. After the attack on Pearl Harbour his family was interned in a civilian camp. They returned to England in 1946. In 1956 Ballard's first story was published in *New Worlds*. His first novel, *The Drowned World*, was published in 1962. *Empire of the Sun*, a novel based on his own experience in China, was published in 1984 and won the *Guardian* Fiction Prize, the James Tait Black Award and was filmed by Steven Spielberg. He is the author of many collections of short stories and novels, including *Cocaine Nights* and *Super-Cannes*.

ALSO BY J. G. BALLARD

*The Drowned World*
*The Voices of Time*
*The Terminal Beach*
*The Drought*
*The Crystal World*
*The Day of Forever*
*The Venus Hunters*
*The Atrocity Exhibition*
*Crash*
*Concrete Island*
*High-Rise*
*Low-Flying Aircraft*
*The Unlimited Dream Company*
*Hello America*
*Myths of the Near Future*
*Empire of the Sun*
*The Day of Creation*
*War Fever*
*Running Wild*
*The Kindness of Women*
*Cocaine Nights*
*Super-Cannes*

J. G. BALLARD

# Vermilion Sands

VINTAGE

15 17 19 20 18 16

Vintage
20 Vauxhall Bridge Road,
London SW1V 2SA

Vintage is part of the Penguin Random House group of companies
whose addresses can be found at global.penguinrandomhouse.com.

This edition reissued by Vintage in 2016
First published in Great Britain by Jonathan Cape in 1973

www.vintage-books.co.uk

A CIP catalogue record for this book is
available from the British Library

ISBN 9780099273585

Printed and bound by Clays Ltd, St Ives plc

# Contents


The Cloud-Sculptors of Coral D 11

Prima Belladonna 31

The Screen Game 47

The Singing Statues 75

Cry Hope, Cry Fury! 91

Venus Smiles 111

Say Goodbye to the Wind 127

Studio 5, The Stars 145

The Thousand Dreams of Stellavista 185

# Preface

Vermilion Sands is my guess at what the future will actually be like. It is a curious paradox that almost all science fiction, however far removed in time and space, is really about the present day. Very few attempts have been made to visualize a unique and self-contained future that offers no warnings to us. Perhaps because of this cautionary tone, so many of science fiction's notional futures are zones of unrelieved grimness. Even its heavens are like other people's hells.

By contrast, Vermilion Sands is a place where I would be happy to live. I once described this overlit desert resort as an exotic suburb of my mind, and something about the word 'suburb' – which I then used pejoratively – now convinces me that I was on the right track in my pursuit of the day after tomorrow. As the countryside vanishes under a top-dressing of chemicals, and as cities provide little more than an urban context for traffic intersections, the suburbs are at last coming into their own. The skies are larger, the air more generous, the clock less urgent. Vermilion Sands has more than its full share of dreams and illusions, fears and fantasies, but the frame for them is less confining. I like to think, too, that it celebrates the neglected virtues of the glossy, lurid and bizarre.

Where is Vermilion Sands? I suppose its spiritual home lies somewhere between Arizona and Ipanema Beach, but in recent years I have been delighted to see it popping up elsewhere – above all, in sections of the 3,000-mile-long linear city that stretches from Gibraltar to Glyfada Beach along the northern shores of the Mediterranean, and where each summer Europe lies on its back in the sun. That posture, of course, is the hallmark of Vermilion Sands and, I hope, of the future – not merely that no-one has to work, but that work is the ultimate play, and play the ultimate work.

The earliest of these tales, 'Prima Belladonna', was the first short story I published, seventeen years ago, and the image of this desert resort has remained remarkably constant ever since. I wait optimistically for it to take concrete shape around me.

J. G. BALLARD

# Vermilion Sands

# The Cloud-Sculptors of Coral D

All summer the cloud-sculptors would come from Vermilion Sands and sail their painted gliders above the coral towers that rose like white pagodas beside the highway to Lagoon West. The tallest of the towers was Coral D, and here the rising air above the sand-reefs was topped by swan-like clumps of fair-weather cumulus. Lifted on the shoulders of the air above the crown of Coral D, we would carve seahorses and unicorns, the portraits of presidents and film stars, lizards and exotic birds. As the crowd watched from their cars, a cool rain would fall on to the dusty roofs, weeping from the sculptured clouds as they sailed across the desert floor towards the sun.

Of all the cloud-sculptures we were to carve, the strangest were the portraits of Leonora Chanel. As I look back to that afternoon last summer when she first came in her white limousine to watch the cloud-sculptors of Coral D, I know we barely realized how seriously this beautiful but insane woman regarded the sculptures floating above her in that calm sky. Later her portraits, carved in the whirlwind, were to weep their storm-rain upon the corpses of their sculptors.

I had arrived in Vermilion Sands three months earlier. A retired pilot, I was painfully coming to terms with a broken leg and the prospect of never flying again. Driving into the desert one day, I stopped near the coral towers on the highway to Lagoon West. As I gazed at these immense pagodas stranded on the floor of this fossil sea, I heard music coming from a sand-reef two hundred yards away. Swinging on my crutches across the sliding sand, I found a shallow basin among the dunes where sonic statues had run to seed beside a ruined studio. The owner had gone, abandoning the hangar-like building to the sand-rays and the desert, and on some half-formed impulse I began to drive out each afternoon. From the lathes and joists left behind I built my first giant kites and, later, gliders with cockpits. Tethered by their cables, they would hang above me in the afternoon air like amiable ciphers.

One evening, as I wound the gliders down on to the winch, a sudden gale rose over the crest of Coral D. While I grappled with the whirling handle, trying to anchor my crutches in the sand, two figures approached across the desert floor. One was a small hunchback with a child's over-lit eyes and a deformed jaw twisted like an anchor barb to one side. He scuttled over to the winch and wound the tattered gliders towards the ground, his powerful shoulders pushing me aside. He helped me on to my crutch and peered into the hangar. Here my most ambitious glider to date, no longer a kite but a sail-plane with elevators and control lines, was taking shape on the bench.

He spread a large hand over his chest. 'Petit Manuel – acrobat and weight-lifter. Nolan!' he bellowed. 'Look at this!' His companion was squatting by the sonic statues, twisting their helixes so that their voices became more resonant. 'Nolan's an artist,' the hunchback confided to me. 'He'll build you gliders like condors.'

The tall man was wandering among the gliders, touching their wings with a sculptor's hand. His morose eyes were set in a face like a bored boxer's. He glanced at the plaster on my leg and my faded flying-jacket, and gestured at the gliders. 'You've given cockpits to them, major.' The remark contained a complete understanding of my motives. He pointed to the coral towers rising above us into the evening sky. 'With silver iodide we could carve the clouds.'

The hunchback nodded encouragingly to me, his eyes lit by an astronomy of dreams.

So were formed the cloud-sculptors of Coral D. Although I considered myself one of them, I never flew the gliders, but taught Nolan and little Manuel to fly, and later, when he joined us, Charles Van Eyck. Nolan had found this blond-haired pirate of the café terraces in Vermilion Sands, a laconic Teuton with hard eyes and a weak mouth, and brought him out to Coral D when the season ended and the well-to-do tourists and their nubile daughters returned to Red Beach. 'Major Parker – Charles Van Eyck. He's a headhunter,' Noland commented with cold humour, '– maidenheads.' Despite their uneasy rivalry I realized that Van Eyck would give our group a useful dimension of glamour.

From the first I suspected that the studio in the desert was Nolan's, and that we were all serving some private whim of this dark-haired solitary. At the time, however, I was more concerned with teaching them to fly – first on cable, mastering the updraughts that swept the stunted turret of Coral A, smallest of the towers, then the steeper slopes of B and C, and finally the powerful currents of Coral D. Late one afternoon, when I began to wind them in, Nolan cut away his line. The glider plummeted on to its back, diving down to impale itself on the rock spires. I flung myself to the ground as the cable whipped across my car, shattering the windshield. When I looked up, Nolan was soaring high in the tinted air above Coral D. The wind, guardian of the coral towers, carried him through the islands of cumulus that veiled the evening light.

As I ran to the winch the second cable went, and little Manuel swerved away to join Nolan. Ugly crab on the ground, in the air the hunchback became a bird with immense wings, outflying both Nolan and Van Eyck. I watched them as they circled the coral towers, and then swept down together over the desert floor, stirring the sand-rays into soot-like clouds. Petit Manuel was jubilant. He strutted around me like a pocket Napoleon, contemptuous of my broken leg, scooping up handfuls of broken glass and tossing them over his head like bouquets to the air.

Two months later, as we drove out to Coral D on the day we were to meet Leonora Chanel, something of this first feeling of exhilaration had faded. Now that the season had ended few tourists travelled to Lagoon West, and often we would perform our cloud-sculpture to the empty highway. Sometimes Nolan would remain behind in his hotel, drinking by himself on the bed, or Van Eyck would disappear for several days with some widow or divorcée, and Petit Manuel and I would go out alone.

None the less, as the four of us drove out in my car that afternoon and I saw the clouds waiting for us above the spire of Coral D, all my depression and fatigue vanished. Ten minutes later, the three cloud-gliders rose into the air and the first cars began to stop on the highway. Nolan was in the lead in his black-winged glider, climbing straight to the crown of Coral D two hundred feet above, while Van Eyck soared to and fro below, showing his blond mane to a middle-aged woman in a topaz convertible. Behind them came little Manuel, his candy-striped wings slipping and churning in the disturbed air. Shouting happy obscenities, he flew with his twisted knees, huge arms gesticulating out of the cockpit.

The three gliders, brilliant painted toys, revolved like lazing birds above Coral D, waiting for the first clouds to pass overhead. Van Eyck moved away to take a cloud. He sailed around its white pillow, spraying the sides with iodide crystals and cutting away the flock-like tissue. The steaming shards fell towards us like crumbling ice-drifts. As the drops of condensing spray fell on my face I could see Van Eyck shaping an immense horse's head. He sailed up and down the long forehead and chiselled out the eyes and ears.

As always, the people watching from their cars seemed to enjoy this piece of aerial marzipan. It sailed overhead, carried away on the wind from Coral D. Van Eyck followed it down, wings lazing around the equine head. Meanwhile Petit Manuel worked away at the next cloud. As he sprayed its sides a familiar human head appeared through the tumbling mist. The high wavy mane, strong jaw but slipped mouth Manuel caricatured from the cloud with a series of deft passes, wingtips almost touching each other as he dived in and out of the portrait.

The glossy white head, an unmistakable parody of Van Eyck in his own worst style, crossed the highway towards Vermilion Sands. Manuel slid out of the air, stalling his glider to a landing beside my car as Van Eyck stepped from his cockpit with a forced smile.

We waited for the third display. A cloud formed over Coral D and within a few minutes had blossomed into a pristine fair-weather cumulus. As it hung there Nolan's black-winged glider plunged out of the sun. He soared around the cloud, cutting away its tissues. The soft fleece fell towards us in a cool rain.

There was a shout from one of the cars. Nolan turned from the cloud, his wings slipping as if unveiling his handiwork. Illuminated by the afternoon sun was the serene face of a three-year-old child. Its wide cheeks framed a placid mouth and plump chin. As one or two people clapped, Nolan sailed over the cloud and rippled the roof into ribbons and curls.

However, I knew that the real climax was yet to come. Cursed by some malignant virus, Nolan seemed unable to accept his own handiwork, always destroying it with the same cold humour. Petit Manuel had thrown away his cigarette, and even Van Eyck had turned his attention from the women in the cars.

Nolan soared above the child's face, following like a matador waiting for the moment of the kill. There was silence for a minute as he worked away at the cloud, and then someone slammed a car door in disgust.

Hanging above us was the white image of a skull.

The child's face, converted by a few strokes, had vanished, but in the notched teeth and gaping orbits, large enough to hold a car, we could still see an echo of its infant features. The spectre moved past us, the spectators frowning at this weeping skull whose rain fell upon their faces.

Half-heartedly I picked my old flying helmet off the back seat and began to carry it around the cars. Two of the spectators drove off before I could reach them. As I hovered about uncertainly, wondering why on earth a retired and well-to-do airforce officer should be trying to collect these few dollar bills, Van Eyck stepped behind me and took the helmet from my hand.

'Not now, major. Look at what arrives – my apocalypse ...'

A white Rolls-Royce, driven by a chauffeur in braided cream livery, had turned off the highway. Through the tinted communication window a young woman in a secretary's day suit spoke to the chauffeur. Beside her, a gloved hand still holding the window strap, a white-haired woman with jewelled eyes gazed up at the circling wings of the cloud-glider. Her strong and elegant face seemed sealed within the dark glass of the limousine like the enigmatic madonna of some marine grotto.

Van Eyck's glider rose into the air, soaring upwards to the cloud that hung above Coral D. I walked back to my car, searching the sky for Nolan. Above, Van Eyck was producing a pastiche Mona Lisa, a picture postcard Gioconda as authentic as a plaster virgin. Its glossy finish shone in the over-bright sunlight as if enamelled together out of some cosmetic foam.

Then Nolan dived from the sun behind Van Eyck. Rolling his black-winged glider past Van Eyck's, he drove through the neck of the Gioconda, and with the flick of a wing toppled the broad-cheeked head. It fell towards the cars below. The features disintegrated into a flaccid mess, sections of the nose and jaw tumbling through the steam. Then wings brushed. Van Eyck fired his spray gun at Nolan, and there was a flurry of torn fabric. Van Eyck fell from the air, steering his glider down to a broken landing.

I ran over to him. 'Charles, do you have to play von Richthofen? For God's sake, leave each other alone!'

Van Eyck waved me away. 'Talk to Nolan, major. I'm not responsible for his air piracy.' He stood in the cockpit, gazing over the cars as the shreds of fabric fell around him.

I walked back to my car, deciding that the time had come to disband the cloud-sculptors of Coral D. Fifty yards away the young secretary in the Rolls-Royce had stepped from the car and beckoned to me. Through the open door her mistress watched me with her jewelled eyes. Her white hair lay in a coil over one shoulder like a nacreous serpent.

I carried my flying helmet down to the young woman. Above a high forehead her auburn hair was swept back in a defensive bun, as if she were deliberately concealing part of herself. She stared with puzzled eyes at the helmet held out in front of her.

'I don't want to fly – what is it?'

'A grace,' I explained. 'For the repose of Michelangelo, Ed Keinholz and the cloud-sculptors of Coral D.'

'Oh, my God. I think the chauffeur's the only one with any *money*. Look, do you perform anywhere else?'

'Perform?' I glanced from this pretty and agreeable young woman to the pale chimera with jewelled eyes in the dim compartment of the Rolls. She was watching the headless figure of the Mona Lisa as it moved across the desert floor towards Vermilion Sands. 'We're not a professional troupe, as you've probably guessed. And obviously we'd need some fair-weather cloud. Where, exactly?'

'At Lagoon West.' She took a snakeskin diary from her handbag. 'Miss Chanel is holding a series of garden parties. She wondered if you'd care to perform. Of course there would be a large fee.'

'Chanel ... Leonora Chanel, the ...?'

The young woman's face again took on its defensive posture, dissociating her from whatever might follow. 'Miss

Chanel is at Lagoon West for the summer. By the way, there's one condition I must point out – Miss Chanel will provide the sole subject matter. You do understand?'

Fifty yards away Van Eyck was dragging his damaged glider towards my car. Nolan had landed, a caricature of Cyrano abandoned in mid-air. Petit Manuel limped to and fro, gathering together the equipment. In the fading afternoon light they resembled a threadbare circus troupe.

'All right,' I agreed. 'I take your point. But what about the clouds, Miss – ?'

'Lafferty. Beatrice Lafferty. Miss Chanel will provide the clouds.'

I walked around the cars with the helmet, then divided the money between Nolan, Van Eyck and Manuel. They stood in the gathering dusk, the few bills in their hands, watching the highway below.

Leonora Chanel stepped from the limousine and strolled into the desert. Her white-haired figure in its cobra-skin coat wandered among the dunes. Sand-rays lifted around her, disturbed by the random movements of this sauntering phantasm of the burnt afternoon. Ignoring their open stings around her legs, she was gazing up at the aerial bestiary dissolving in the sky, and at the white skull a mile away over Lagoon West that had smeared itself across the sky.

At the time I first saw her, watching the cloud-sculptors of Coral D, I had only a half-formed impression of Leonora Chanel. The daughter of one of the world's leading financiers, she was an heiress both in her own right and on the death of her husband, a shy Monacan aristocrat, Comte Louis Chanel. The mysterious circumstances of his death at Cap Ferrat on the Riviera, officially described as suicide, had placed Leonora in a spotlight of publicity and gossip. She had escaped by wandering endlessly across the globe, from her walled villa in

Tangiers to an Alpine mansion in the snows above Pontresina, and from there to Palm Springs, Seville and Mykonos.

During these years of exile something of her character emerged from the magazine and newspaper photographs: moodily visiting a Spanish charity with the Duchess of Alba, or seated with Soraya and other members of café society on the terrace of Dali's villa at Port Lligat, her self-regarding face gazing out with its jewelled eyes at the diamond sea of the Costa Brava.

Inevitably her Garbo-like role seemed over-calculated, for ever undermined by the suspicions of her own hand in her husband's death. The count had been an introspective playboy who piloted his own aircraft to archaeological sites in the Peloponnese and whose mistress, a beautiful young Lebanese, was one of the world's pre-eminent keyboard interpreters of Bach. Why this reserved and pleasant man should have committed suicide was never made plain. What promised to be a significant exhibit at the coroner's inquest, a mutilated easel portrait of Leonora on which he was working, was accidentally destroyed before the hearing. Perhaps the painting revealed more of Leonora's character than she chose to see.

A week later, as I drove out to Lagoon West on the morning of the first garden party, I could well understand why Leonora Chanel had come to Vermilion Sands, to this bizarre, sand-bound resort with its lethargy, beach fatigue and shifting perspectives. Sonic statues grew wild along the beach, their voices keening as I swept past along the shore road. The fused silica on the surface of the lake formed an immense rainbow mirror that reflected the deranged colours of the sand-reefs, more vivid even than the cinnabar and cyclamen wing-panels of the cloud-gliders overhead. They soared in the sky above the lake like fitful dragonflies as Nolan, Van Eyck and Petit Manuel flew them from Coral D.

We had entered an inflamed landscape. Half a mile away

the angular cornices of the summer house jutted into the vivid air as if distorted by some faulty junction of time and space. Behind it, like an exhausted volcano, a broad-topped mesa rose into the glazed air, its shoulders lifting the thermal currents high off the heated lake.

Envying Nolan and little Manuel these tremendous up-draughts, more powerful than any we had known at Coral D, I drove towards the villa. Then the haze cleared along the beach and I saw the clouds.

A hundred feet above the roof of the mesa, they hung like the twisted pillows of a sleepless giant. Columns of turbulent air moved within the clouds, boiling upwards to the anvil heads like liquid in a cauldron. These were not the placid, fair-weather cumulus of Coral D, but storm-nimbus, unstable masses of overheated air that could catch an aircraft and lift it a thousand feet in a few seconds. Here and there the clouds were rimmed with dark bands, their towers crossed by valleys and ravines. They moved across the villa, concealed from the lakeside heat by the haze overhead, then dissolved in a series of violent shifts in the disordered air.

As I entered the drive behind a truck filled with *son et lumière* equipment a dozen members of the staff were straight-ening lines of gilt chairs on the terrace and unrolling panels of a marquee.

Beatrice Lafferty stepped across the cables. 'Major Parker – there are the clouds we promised you.'

I looked up again at the dark billows hanging like shrouds above the white villa. 'Clouds, Beatrice? Those are tigers, tigers with wings. We're manicurists of the air, not dragon-tamers.'

'Don't worry, a manicure is exactly what you're expected to carry out.' With an arch glance, she added: 'Your men do understand that there's to be only one subject?'

'Miss Chanel herself? Of course.' I took her arm as we walked towards the balcony overlooking the lake. 'You know, I think you enjoy these snide asides. Let the rich choose their materials – marble, bronze, plasma or cloud. Why not? Portraiture has always been a neglected art.'

'My God, not here.' She waited until a steward passed with a tray of tablecloths. 'Carving one's portrait in the sky out of the sun and air – some people might say that smacked of vanity, or even worse sins.'

'You're very mysterious. Such as?'

She played games with her eyes. 'I'll tell you in a month's time when my contract expires. Now, when are your men coming?'

'They're here.' I pointed to the sky over the lake. The three gliders hung in the overheated air, clumps of cloud-cotton drifting past them to dissolve in the haze. They were following a sand-yacht that approached the quay, its tyres throwing up the cerise dust. Behind the helmsman sat Leonora Chanel in a trouser suit of yellow alligator skin, her white hair hidden inside a black raffia toque.

As the helmsman moored the craft Van Eyck and Petit Manuel put on an impromptu performance, shaping the fragments of cloud-cotton a hundred feet above the lake. First Van Eyck carved an orchid, then a heart and a pair of lips, while Manuel fashioned the head of a parakeet, two identical mice and the letters 'L.C.' As they dived and plunged around her, their wings sometimes touching the lake, Leonora stood on the quay, politely waving at each of these brief confections.

When they landed beside the quay, Leonora waited for Nolan to take one of the clouds, but he was sailing up and down the lake in front of her like a weary bird. Watching this strange chatelaine of Lagoon West, I noticed that she had slipped off into some private reverie, her gaze fixed on Nolan and oblivious of the people around her. Memories, caravels without sails, crossed the shadowy deserts of her burnt-out eyes.

Later that evening Beatrice Lafferty led me into the villa through the library window. There, as Leonora greeted her guests on the terrace, wearing a topless dress of sapphires and organdy, her breasts covered only by their contour jewellery, I saw the portraits that filled the villa. I counted more than twenty, from the formal society portraits in the drawing rooms, one by the President of the Royal Academy, another by Annigoni, to the bizarre psychological studies in the bar and dining room by Dali and Francis Bacon. Everywhere we moved, in the alcoves between the marble semi-columns, in gilt miniatures on the mantel shelves, even in the ascending mural that followed the staircase, we saw the same beautiful self-regarding face. This colossal narcissism seemed to have become her last refuge, the only retreat for her fugitive self in its flight from the world.

Then, in the studio on the roof, we came across a large easel portrait that had just been varnished. The artist had produced a deliberate travesty of the sentimental and powder-blue tints of a fashionable society painter, but beneath this gloss he had visualized Leonora as a dead Medea. The stretched skin below her right cheek, the sharp forehead and slipped mouth gave her the numbed and luminous appearance of a corpse.

My eyes moved to the signature. 'Nolan! My God, were you here when he painted this?'

'It was finished before I came – two months ago. She refused to have it framed.'

'No wonder.' I went over to the window and looked down at the bedrooms hidden behind their awnings. 'Nolan was *here*. The old studio near Coral D was his.'

'But why should Leonora ask him back? They must have –'

'To paint her portrait again. I know Leonora Chanel better than you do, Beatrice. This time, though, the size of the sky.'

We left the library and walked past the cocktails and canapés to where Leonora was welcoming her guests. Nolan stood beside her, wearing a suit of white suede. Now and then he looked down at her as if playing with the possibilities this self-obsessed woman gave to his macabre humour. Leonora clutched at his elbow. With the diamonds fixed around her eyes she reminded me of some archaic priestess. Beneath the contour jewellery her breasts lay like eager snakes.

Van Eyck introduced himself with an exaggerated bow. Behind him came Petit Manuel, his twisted head ducking nervously among the tuxedos.

Leonora's mouth shut in a rictus of distaste. She glanced at the white plaster on my foot. 'Nolan, you fill your world with cripples. Your little dwarf – will he fly too?'

Petit Manuel looked at her with eyes like crushed flowers.

The performance began an hour later. The dark-rimmed clouds were lit by the sun setting behind the mesa, the air crossed by wraiths of cirrus like the gilded frames of the immense paintings to come. Van Eyck's glider rose in the spiral towards the face of the first cloud, stalling and climbing again as the turbulent updraughts threw him across the air.

As the cheekbones began to appear, as smooth and lifeless as carved foam, applause rang out from the guests seated on the terrace. Five minutes later, when Van Eyck's glider swooped down on to the lake, I could see that he had excelled himself. Lit by the searchlights, and with the overture to Tristan sounding from the loudspeakers on the slopes of the mesa, as if inflating this huge bauble, the portrait of Leonora moved overhead, a faint rain falling from it. By luck the cloud remained stable until it passed the shoreline, and then broke up in the evening air as if ripped from the sky by an irritated hand.

Petit Manuel began his ascent, sailing in on a dark-edged cloud like an urchin accosting a bad-tempered matron. He soared to and fro, as if unsure how to shape this unpredictable column of vapour, then began to carve it into the approximate contours of a woman's head. He seemed more nervous than I had ever seen him. As he finished a second round of applause broke out, soon followed by laughter and ironic cheers.

The cloud, sculptured into a flattering likeness of Leonora, had begun to tilt, rotating in the disturbed air. The jaw lengthened, the glazed smile became that of an idiot's. Within a minute the gigantic head of Leonora Chanel hung upside down above us.

Discreetly I ordered the searchlights switched off, and the audience's attention turned to Nolan's black-winged glider as it climbed towards the next cloud. Shards of dissolving tissue fell from the darkening air, the spray concealing whatever ambiguous creation Nolan was carving. To my surprise, the portrait that emerged was wholly lifelike. There was a burst of applause, a few bars of Tannhauser, and the searchlights lit up the elegant head. Standing among her guests, Leonora raised her glass to Nolan's glider.

Puzzled by Nolan's generosity, I looked more closely at the gleaming face, and then realized what he had done. The portrait, with cruel irony, was all too lifelike. The downward turn of Leonora's mouth, the chin held up to smooth her neck, the fall of flesh below her right cheek – all these were carried on the face of the cloud as they had been in his painting in the studio.

Around Leonora the guests were congratulating her on the performance. She was looking up at her portrait as it began to break up over the lake, seeing it for the first time. The veins held the blood in her face.

Then a firework display on the beach blotted out these ambiguities in its pink and blue explosions.

Shortly before dawn Beatrice Lafferty and I walked along the beach among the shells of burnt-out rockets and catherine wheels. On the deserted terrace a few lights shone through the darkness on to the scattered chairs. As we reached the steps a woman's voice cried out somewhere above us. There was the sound of smashed glass. A french window was kicked back, and a dark-haired man in a white suit ran between the tables.

As Nolan disappeared along the drive Leonora Chanel walked out into the centre of the terrace. She looked at the dark clouds surging over the mesa, and with one hand tore the jewels from her eyes. They lay winking on the tiles at her feet. Then the hunched figure of Petit Manuel leapt from his hiding place in the bandstand. He scuttled past, racing on his deformed legs.

An engine started by the gates. Leonora began to walk back to the villa, staring at her broken reflections in the glass below the window. She stopped as a tall, blond-haired man with cold and eager eyes stepped from the sonic statues outside the library. Disturbed by the noise, the statues had begun to whine. As Van Eyck moved towards Leonora they took up the slow beat of his steps.

The next day's performance was the last by the cloud-sculptors of Coral D. All afternoon, before the guests arrived, a dim light lay over the lake. Immense tiers of storm-nimbus were massing behind the mesa, and any performance at all seemed unlikely.

Van Eyck was with Leonora. As I arrived Beatrice Lafferty was watching their sand-yacht carry them unevenly across the lake, its sails whipped by the squalls.

'There's no sign of Nolan or little Manuel,' she told me. 'The party starts in three hours.'

I took her arm. 'The party's already over. When you're finished here, Bea, come and live with me at Coral D. I'll teach you to sculpt the clouds.'

Van Eyck and Leonora came ashore half an hour later. Van Eyck stared through my face as he brushed past. Leonora clung to his arm, the day-jewels around her eyes scattering their hard light across the terrace.

By eight, when the first guests began to appear, Nolan and Petit Manuel had still not arrived. On the terrace the evening was warm and lamplit, but overhead the storm-clouds sidled past each other like uneasy giants. I walked up the slope to where the gliders were tethered. Their wings shivered in the updraughts.

Barely half a minute after he rose into the darkening air, dwarfed by an immense tower of storm-nimbus, Charles Van Eyck was spinning towards the ground, his glider toppled by the crazed air. He recovered fifty feet from the villa and climbed on the updraughts from the lake, well away from the spreading chest of the cloud. He soared in again. As Leonora and her guests watched from their seats the glider was hurled back over their heads in an explosion of vapour, then fell towards the lake with a broken wing.

I walked towards Leonora. Standing by the balcony were Nolan and Petit Manuel, watching Van Eyck climb from the cockpit of his glider three hundred yards away.

To Nolan I said: 'Why bother to come? Don't tell me you're going to fly?'

Nolan leaned against the rail, hands in the pockets of his suit. 'I'm not – that's exactly why I'm here, major.'

Leonora was wearing an evening dress of peacock feathers that lay around her legs in an immense train. The hundreds of eyes gleamed in the electric air before the storm, sheathing her body in their blue flames.

'Miss Chanel, the clouds are like madmen,' I apologized. 'There's a storm on its way.'

She looked up at me with unsettled eyes. 'Don't you people expect to take risks?' She gestured at the storm-nimbus that swirled over our heads. 'For clouds like these I need a Michelangelo of the sky ... What about Nolan? Is he too frightened as well?'

As she shouted his name Nolan stared at her, then turned his back to us. The light over Lagoon West had changed. Half the lake was covered by a dim pall.

There was a tug on my sleeve. Petit Manuel looked up at me

with his crafty child's eyes. 'Major, I can go. Let me take the glider.'

'Manuel, for God's sake. You'll kill –'

He darted between the gilt chairs. Leonora frowned as he plucked her wrist.

'Miss Chanel ...' His loose mouth formed an encouraging smile. 'I'll sculpt for you. Right now, a big storm-cloud, eh?'

She stared down at him, half-repelled by this eager hunchback ogling her beside the hundred eyes of her peacock train. Van Eyck was limping back to the beach from his wrecked glider. I guessed that in some strange way Manuel was pitting himself against Van Eyck.

Leonora grimaced, as if swallowing some poisonous phlegm. 'Major Parker, tell him to –' She glanced at the dark cloud boiling over the mesa like the effluvium of some black-hearted volcano. 'Wait! Let's see what the little cripple can do!' She turned on Manuel with an over-bright smile. 'Go on, then. Let's see you sculpt a whirlwind!'

In her face the diagram of bones formed a geometry of murder.

Nolan ran past across the terrace, his feet crushing the peacock feathers as Leonora laughed. We tried to stop Manuel, but he raced ahead up the slope. Stung by Leonora's taunt, he skipped among the rocks, disappearing from sight in the darkening air. On the terrace a small crowd gathered to watch.

The yellow and tangerine glider rose into the sky and climbed across the face of the storm-cloud. Fifty yards from the dark billows it was buffeted by the shifting air, but Manuel soared in and began to cut away at the dark face. Drops of black rain fell across the terrace at our feet.

The first outline of a woman's head appeared, satanic eyes lit by the open vents in the cloud, a sliding mouth like a dark smear as the huge billows boiled forwards. Nolan shouted in warning from the lake as he climbed into his glider. A moment later little Manuel's craft was lifted by a powerful updraught and tossed over the roof of the cloud. Fighting the insane air, Manuel plunged the glider downwards and drove into the cloud again. Then its immense face opened, and in a sudden spasm the cloud surged forward and swallowed the glider.

There was silence on the terrace as the crushed body of the craft revolved in the centre of the cloud. It moved over our heads, dismembered pieces of the wings and fuselage churned about in the dissolving face. As it reached the lake the cloud began its violent end. Pieces of the face slewed sideways, the mouth was torn off, an eye exploded. It vanished in a last brief squall.

The pieces of Petit Manuel's glider fell from the bright air.

Beatrice Lafferty and I drove across the lake to collect Manuel's body. After the spectacle of his death within the exploding replica of their hostess's face, the guests began to leave. Within minutes the drive was full of cars. Leonora watched them go, standing with Van Eyck among the deserted tables.

Beatrice said nothing as we drove out. The pieces of the shattered glider lay over the fused sand, tags of canvas and broken struts, control lines tied into knots. Ten yards from the cockpit I found Petit Manuel's body, lying in a wet ball like a drowned monkey.

I carried him back to the sand-yacht.

'Raymond!' Beatrice pointed to the shore. Storm-clouds were massed along the entire length of the lake, and the first flashes of lightning were striking in the hills behind the mesa. In the electric air the villa had lost its glitter. Half a mile away a tornado was moving along the valley floor, its trunk swaying towards the lake.

The first gust of air struck the yacht. Beatrice shouted again: 'Raymond! Nolan's there – he's flying inside it!'

Then I saw the black-winged glider circling under the umbrella of the tornado, Nolan himself riding in the whirlwind. His wings held steady in the revolving air around the funnel.

Like a pilot fish he soared in, as if steering the tornado towards Leonora's villa.

Twenty seconds later, when it struck the house, I lost sight of him. An explosion of dark air overwhelmed the villa, a churning centrifuge of shattered chairs and tiles that burst over the roof. Beatrice and I ran from the yacht, and lay together in a fault in the glass surface. As the tornado moved away, fading into the storm-filled sky, a dark squall hung over the wrecked villa, now and then flicking the debris into the air. Shreds of canvas and peacock feathers fell around us.

We waited half an hour before approaching the house. Hundreds of smashed glasses and broken chairs littered the terrace. At first I could see no signs of Leonora, although her face was everywhere, the portraits with their slashed profiles strewn on the damp tiles. An eddying smile floated towards me from the disturbed air, and wrapped itself around my leg.

Leonora's body lay among the broken tables near the bandstand, half-wrapped in a bleeding canvas. Her face was as bruised now as the storm-cloud Manuel had tried to carve.

We found Van Eyck in the wreck of the marquee. He was suspended by the neck from a tangle of electric wiring, his pale face wreathed in a noose of light bulbs. The current flowed intermittently through the wiring, lighting up the coloured globes.

I leaned against the overturned Rolls, holding Beatrice's shoulders. 'There's no sign of Nolan – no pieces of his glider.'

'Poor man. Raymond, he was driving that whirlwind here. Somehow he was controlling it.'

I walked across the damp terrace to where Leonora lay. I began to cover her with the shreds of canvas, the torn faces of herself.

I took Beatrice Lafferty to live with me in Nolan's studio in the desert near Coral D. We heard no more of Nolan and never flew the gliders again. The clouds carry too many memories. Three months ago a man who saw the derelict gliders outside the studio stopped near Coral D and walked across to us. He told us he had seen a man flying a glider in the sky high above Red Beach, carving the strato-cirrus into images of jewels and children's faces. Once there was a dwarf's head.

On reflection, that sounds rather like Nolan, so perhaps he managed to get away from the tornado. In the evenings Beatrice and I sit among the sonic statues, listening to their voices as the fair-weather clouds rise above Coral D, waiting for a man in a dark-winged glider, perhaps painted like candy now, who will come in on the wind and carve for us images of seahorses and unicorns, dwarfs and jewels and children's faces.

# Prima Belladonna

I first met Jane Ciracylides during the Recess, that world slump of boredom, lethargy and high summer which carried us all so blissfully through ten unforgettable years, and I suppose that may have had a lot to do with what went on between us. Certainly I can't believe I could make myself as ridiculous now, but then again, it might have been just Jane herself.

Whatever else they said about her, everyone had to agree she was a beautiful girl, even if her genetic background was a little mixed. The gossips at Vermilion Sands soon decided there was a good deal of mutant in her, because she had a rich patina-golden skin and what looked like insects for eyes, but that didn't bother either myself or any of my friends, one or two of whom, like Tony Miles and Harry Devine, have never since been quite the same to their wives.

We spent most of our time in those days on the balcony of my apartment off Beach Drive, drinking beer – we always kept a useful supply stacked in the refrigerator of my music shop on the street level – yarning in a desultory way and playing i-Go, a sort of decelerated chess which was popular then. None of the others ever did any work; Harry was an architect and Tony Miles sometimes sold a few ceramics to the tourists, but I usually put a couple of hours in at the shop each morning, getting off the foreign orders and turning the beer.

One particularly hot lazy day I'd just finished wrapping up a delicate soprano mimosa wanted by the Hamburg Oratorio Society when Harry phoned down from the balcony.

'Parker's Choro-Flora?' he said. 'You're guilty of overproduction. Come up here. Tony and I have something beautiful to show you.'

When I went up I found them grinning happily like two dogs who had just discovered an interesting tree.

'Well?' I asked. 'Where is it?'

Tony tilted his head slightly. 'Over there.'

I looked up and down the street, and across the face of the apartment house opposite.

'Careful,' he warned me. 'Don't gape at her.'

I slid into one of the wicker chairs and craned my head round cautiously.

'Fourth floor,' Harry elaborated slowly, out of the side of his mouth. 'One left from the balcony opposite. Happy now?'

'Dreaming,' I told him, taking a long slow focus on her. 'I wonder what else she can do?'

Harry and Tony sighed thankfully. 'Well?' Tony asked.

'She's out of my league,' I said. 'But you two shouldn't have any trouble. Go over and tell her how much she needs you.'

Harry groaned. 'Don't you realize, this one is poetic, emergent, something straight out of the primal apocalyptic sea. She's probably divine.'

The woman was strolling around the lounge, rearranging the furniture, wearing almost nothing except a large metallic hat. Even in shadow the sinuous lines of her thighs and shoulders gleamed gold and burning. She was a walking galaxy of light. Vermilion Sands had never seen anything like her.

'The approach has got to be equivocal,' Harry continued, gazing into his beer. 'Shy, almost mystical. Nothing urgent or grabbing.'

The woman stooped down to unpack a suitcase and the metal vanes of her hat fluttered over her face. She saw us staring at her, looked around for a moment and lowered the blinds.

We sat back and looked thoughtfully at each other, like three triumvirs deciding how to divide an empire, not saying too much, and one eye watching for any chance of a double-deal.

Five minutes later the singing started.

At first I thought it was one of the azalea trios in trouble with an alkaline pH, but the frequencies were too high. They were almost out of the audible range, a thin tremolo quaver which came out of nowhere and rose up the back of the skull.

Harry and Tony frowned at me.

'Your livestock's unhappy about something,' Tony told me. 'Can you quieten it down?'

'It's not the plants,' I told him. 'Can't be.'

The sound mounted in intensity, scraping the edges oft my occipital bones. I was about to go down to the shop when Harry and Tony leapt out of their chairs and dived back against the wall.

'Steve, look out!' Tony yelled at me. He pointed wildly at the table I was leaning on, picked up a chair and smashed it down on the glass top.

I stood up and brushed the fragments out of my hair.

'What the hell's the matter?'

Tony was looking down at the tangle of wickerwork tied round the metal struts of the table. Harry came forward and took my arm gingerly.

'That was close. You all right?'

'It's gone,' Tony said flatly. He looked carefully over the balcony floor and down over the rail into the street.

'What was it?' I asked.

Harry peered at me closely. 'Didn't you see it? It was about three inches from you. Emperor scorpion, big as a lobster.' He sat down weakly on a beer crate. 'Must have been a sonic one. The noise has gone now.'

After they'd left I cleared up the mess and had a quiet beer to myself. I could have sworn nothing had got on to the table.

On the balcony opposite, wearing a gown of ionized fibre, the golden woman was watching me.

I found out who she was the next morning. Tony and Harry were down at the beach with their wives, probably enlarging on the scorpion, and I was in the shop tuning up a Khan-Arachnid orchid with the UV lamp. It was a difficult bloom, with a normal full range of twenty-four octaves, but unless it got a lot of exercise it tended to relapse into neurotic minor-key transpositions which were the devil to break. And as the senior bloom in the shop it naturally affected all the others. Invariably when I opened the shop in the mornings, it sounded like a madhouse, but as soon as I'd fed the Arachnid and straightened out one or two pH gradients the rest promptly took their cues from it and dimmed down quietly in their control tanks, two-time, three-four, the multi-tones, all in perfect harmony.

There were only about a dozen true Arachnids in captivity; most of the others were either mutes or grafts from dicot stems, and I was lucky to have mine at all. I'd bought the place five years earlier from an old half-deaf man called Sayers, and the day before he left he moved a lot of rogue stock out to the garbage disposal scoop behind the apartment block. Reclaiming some of the tanks I'd come across the Arachnid, thriving on a diet of algae and perished rubber tubing.

Why Sayers had wanted to throw it away I had never discovered. Before he came to Vermilion Sands he'd been a curator at the Kew Conservatoire where the first choro-flora had been bred, and had worked under the Director, Dr Mandel. As a young botanist of twenty-five Mandel had discovered the prime Arachnid in the Guiana forest. The orchid took its name from the Khan-Arachnid spider which pollinated the flower, simultaneously laying its own eggs in the fleshy ovule, guided, or as Mandel always insisted, actually mesmerized to it by the vibrations which the orchid's calyx emitted at pollination time. The first Arachnid orchids beamed out only a few random frequencies, but by cross-breeding and maintaining them artificially at the pollination stage Mandel had produced a strain that spanned a maximum of twenty-four octaves.

Not that he had ever been able to hear them. At the climax of his life's work Mandel, like Beethoven, was stone deaf, but apparently by merely looking at a blossom he could listen to its music. Strangely though, after he went deaf he never looked at an Arachnid.

That morning I could almost understand why. The orchid was in a vicious mood. First it refused to feed, and I had to coax it along in a fluoraldehyde flush, and then it started going ultra-sonic, which meant complaints from all the dog owners in the area. Finally it tried to fracture the tank by resonating.

The whole place was in uproar, and I was almost resigned to shutting them down and waking them all by hand individually – a backbreaking job with eighty tanks in the shop – when everything suddenly died away to a murmur.

I looked round and saw the golden-skinned woman walk in.

'Good morning,' I said. 'They must like you.'

She laughed pleasantly. 'Hello. Weren't they behaving?'

Under the black beach robe her skin was a softer, more mellow gold, and it was her eyes that held me. I could just see them under the wide-brimmed hat. Insect legs wavered delicately round two points of purple light.

She walked over to a bank of mixed ferns and stood looking at them. The ferns reached out towards her and trebled eagerly in their liquid fluted voices.

'Aren't they sweet?' she said, stroking the fronds gently. 'They need so much affection.'

Her voice was low in the register, a breath of cool sand pouring, with a lilt that gave it music.

'I've just come to Vermilion Sands,' she said, 'and my apartment seems awfully quiet. Perhaps if I had a flower, one would be enough, I shouldn't feel so lonely.'

I couldn't take my eyes off her.

'Yes,' I agreed, brisk and businesslike. 'What about something colourful? This Sumatra Samphire, say? It's a pedigree mezzo-soprano from the same follicle as the Bayreuth Festival Prima Belladonna.'

'No,' she said. 'It looks rather cruel.'

'Or this Louisiana Lute Lily? If you thin out its $SO_2$ it'll play some beautiful madrigals. I'll show you how to do it.'

She wasn't listening to me. Slowly, her hands raised in front of her breasts so that she almost seemed to be praying, she moved towards the display counter on which the Arachnid stood.

'How beautiful it is,' she said, gazing at the rich yellow and purple leaves hanging from the scarlet-ribbed vibrocalyx.

I followed her across the floor and switched on the Arachnid's audio so that she could hear it. Immediately the plant came to life. The leaves stiffened and filled with colour and the calyx inflated, its ribs sprung tautly. A few sharp disconnected notes spat out.

'Beautiful, but evil,' I said.

'Evil?' she repeated. 'No, proud.' She stepped closer to the orchid and looked down into its malevolent head. The Arachnid quivered and the spines on its stem arched and flexed menacingly.

'Careful,' I warned her. 'It's sensitive to the faintest respiratory sounds.'

'Quiet,' she said, waving me back. 'I think it wants to sing.'

'Those are only key fragments,' I told her. 'It doesn't perform. I use it as a frequency –'

'Listen!' She held my arm and squeezed it tightly.

A low, rhythmic fusion of melody had been coming from the plants around the shop, and mounting above them I heard a single stronger voice calling out, at first a thin high-pitched reed of sound that began to pulse and deepen and finally swelled into full baritone, raising the other plants in chorus about itself.

I had never heard the Arachnid sing before. I was listening to it open-eared when I felt a glow of heat burn against my arm. I turned and saw the woman staring intently at the plant, her skin aflame, the insects in her eyes writhing insanely. The Arachnid stretched out towards her, calyx erect, leaves like blood-red sabres.

I stepped round her quickly and switched off the argon feed. The Arachnid sank to a whimper, and around us there was a nightmarish babel of broken notes and voices toppling from high C's and L's into discord. A faint whispering of leaves moved over the silence.

The woman gripped the edge of the tank and gathered herself. Her skin dimmed and the insects in her eyes slowed to a delicate wavering.

'Why did you turn it off?' she asked heavily.

'I'm sorry,' I said. 'But I've got ten thousand dollars' worth of stock here and that sort of twelve-tone emotional storm can blow a lot of valves. Most of these plants aren't equipped for grand opera.'

She watched the Arachnid as the gas drained out of its calyx. One by one its leaves buckled and lost their colour.

'How much is it?' she asked me, opening her bag.

'It's not for sale,' I said. 'Frankly I've no idea how it picked up those bars –'

'Will a thousand dollars be enough?' she asked, her eyes fixed on me steadily.

'I can't,' I told her. 'I'd never be able to tune the others without it. Anyway,' I added, trying to smile, 'that Arachmid would be dead in ten minutes if you took it out of its vivarium. All these cylinders and leads would look a little odd inside your lounge.'

'Yes, of course,' she agreed, suddenly smiling back at me. 'I was stupid.' She gave the orchid a last backward glance and strolled away across the floor to the long Tchaikovsky section popular with the tourists.

'*Pathétique*,' she read off a label at random. 'I'll take this.'

I wrapped up the scabia and slipped the instructional booklet into the crate, keeping my eye on her all the time.

'Don't look so alarmed,' she said with amusement. 'I've never heard anything like that before.'

I wasn't alarmed. It was that thirty years at Vermilion Sands had narrowed my horizons.

'How long are you staying at Vermilion Sands?' I asked her.

'I open at the Casino tonight,' she said. She told me her name was Jane Ciracylides and that she was a speciality singer.

'Why don't you look in?' she asked, her eyes fluttering mischievously. 'I come on at eleven. You may find it interesting.'

I did. The next morning Vermilion Sands hummed. Jane created a sensation. After her performance three hundred people swore they'd seen everything from a choir of angels taking the vocal in the music of the spheres to Alexander's Ragtime Band. As for myself, perhaps I'd listened to too many flowers, but at least I knew where the scorpion on the balcony had come from.

Tony Miles had heard Sophie Tucker singing the 'St Louis Blues', and Harry, the elder Bach conducting the B Minor Mass.

They came round to the shop and argued over their respective performances while I wrestled with the flowers.

'Amazing,' Tony exclaimed. 'How does she do it? Tell me.'

'The Heidelberg score,' Harry ecstased. 'Sublime, absolute.' He looked irritably at the flowers. 'Can't you keep these things quiet? They're making one hell of a row.'

They were, and I had a shrewd idea why. The Arachnid was

completely out of control, and by the time I'd clamped it down in a weak saline it had blown out over three hundred dollars' worth of shrubs.

'The performance at the Casino last night was nothing on the one she gave here yesterday,' I told them. '*The Ring of the Niebelungs* played by Stan Kenton. That Arachnid went insane. I'm sure it wanted to kill her.'

Harry watched the plant convulsing its leaves in rigid spasmic movements.

'If you ask me it's in an advanced state of rut. Why should it want to kill her?'

'Her voice must have overtones that irritate its calyx. None of the other plants minded. They cooed like turtle doves when she touched them.'

Tony shivered happily.

Light dazzled in the street outside.

I handed Tony the broom. 'Here, lover, brace yourself on that. Miss Ciracylides is dying to meet you.'

Jane came into the shop, wearing a flame yellow cocktail skirt and another of her hats.

I introduced her to Harry and Tony.

'The flowers seem very quiet this morning,' she said. 'What's the matter with them?'

'I'm cleaning out the tanks,' I told her. 'By the way, we all want to congratulate you on last night. How does it feel to be able to name your fiftieth city?'

She smiled shyly and sauntered away round the shop. As I knew she would, she stopped by the Arachnid and levelled her eyes at it.

I wanted to see what she'd say, but Harry and Tony were all around her, and soon got her up to my apartment, where they had a hilarious morning playing the fool and raiding my Scotch.

'What about coming out with us after the show tonight?' Tony asked her. 'We can go dancing at the Flamingo.'

'But you're both married,' Jane protested. 'Aren't you worried about your reputations?'

'Oh, we'll bring the girls,' Harry said airily. 'And Steve here can come along and hold your coat.'

We played i-Go together. Jane said she'd never played the game before, but she had no difficulty picking up the rules, and when she started sweeping the board with us I knew she was cheating. Admittedly it isn't every day that you get a chance to play i-Go with a golden-skinned woman with insects for eyes, but never the less I was annoyed. Harry and Tony, of course, didn't mind.

'She's charming,' Harry said. after she'd left. 'Who cares? It's a stupid game anyway.'

'I care,' I said. 'She cheats.'

The next three or four days at the shop were an audio-vegetative armageddon. Jane came in every morning to look at the Arachnid, and her presence was more than the flower could bear. Unfortunately I couldn't starve the plants below their thresholds. They needed exercise and they had to have the Arachnid to lead them. But instead of running through its harmonic scales the orchid only screeched and whined. It wasn't the noise, which only a couple of dozen people complained about, but the damage being done to their vibratory chords that worried me. Those in the seventeenth century catalogues stood up well to the strain, and the moderns were immune, but the Romantics burst their calyxes by the score. By the third day after Jane's arrival I'd lost two hundred dollars' worth of Beethoven and more Mendelssohn and Schubert than I could bear to think about.

Jane seemed oblivous to the trouble she was causing me.

'What's wrong with them all?' she asked, surveying the chaos of gas cylinders and drip feeds spread across the floor.

'I don't think they like you,' I told her. 'At least the Arachnid doesn't. Your voice may move men to strange and wonderful visions, but it throws that orchid into acute melancholia.'

'Nonsense,' she said, laughing at me. 'Give it to me and I'll show you how to look after it.'

'Are Tony and Harry keeping you happy?' I asked her. I was annoyed that I couldn't go down to the beach with them and instead had to spend my time draining tanks and titrating up norm solutions, none of which ever worked.

'They're very amusing,' she said. 'We play i-Go and I sing for them. But I wish you could come out more often.'

After another two weeks I had to give up. I decided to close the plants down until Jane had left Vermilion Sands. I knew it would take me three months to rescore the stock, but I had no alternative.

The next day I received a large order for mixed coloratura herbaceous from the Santiago Garden Choir. They wanted delivery in three weeks.

'I'm sorry,' Jane said, when she heard I wouldn't be able to fill the order. 'You must wish that I'd never come to Vermilion Sands.'

She stared thoughtfully into one of the darkened tanks.

'Couldn't I score them for you?' she suggested.

'No thanks,' I said, laughing. 'I've had enough of that already.'

'Don't be silly, of course I could.'

I shook my head.

Tony and Harry told me I was crazy.

'Her voice has a wide enough range,' Tony said. 'You admit it yourself.'

'What have you got against her?' Harry asked. 'That she cheats at i-Go?'

'It's nothing to do with that,' I said. 'And her voice has a wider range than you think.'

We played i-Go at Jane's apartment. Jane won ten dollars from each of us.

'I am lucky,' she said, very pleased with herself. 'I never seem to lose.' She counted up the bills and put them away carefully in her bag, her golden skin glowing.

Then Santiago sent me a repeat query.

I found Jane down among the cafés, holding off a siege of admirers.

'Have you given in yet?' she asked me, smiling at the young men.

'I don't know what you're doing to me,' I said, 'but anything is worth trying.'

Back at the shop I raised a bank of perennials past their thresholds. Jane helped me attach the gas and fluid lines.

'We'll try these first,' I said. 'Frequencies 543–785. Here's the score.'

Jane took off her hat and began to ascend the scale, her voice clear and pure. At first the Columbine hesitated and Jane went down again and drew them along with her. They went up a couple of octaves together and then the plants stumbled and went off at a tangent of stepped chords.

'Try K sharp,' I said. I fed a little chlorous acid into the tank and the Columbine followed her up eagerly, the infra-calyxes warbling delicate variations on the treble clef.

'Perfect,' I said.

It took us only four hours to fill the order.

'You're better than the Arachnid,' I congratulated her. 'How would you like a job? I'll fit you out with a large cool tank and all the chlorine you can breathe.'

'Careful,' she told me. 'I may say yes. Why don't we rescore a few more of them while we're about it?'

'You're tired,' I said. 'Let's go and have a drink.'

'Let me try the Arachnid,' she suggested. 'That would be more of a challenge.'

Her eyes never left the flower. I wondered what they'd do if I left them together. Try to sing each other to death?

'No,' I said. 'Tomorrow perhaps.'

We sat on the balcony together, glasses at our elbows, and talked the afternoon away.

She told me little about herself, but I gathered that her father had been a mining engineer in Peru and her mother a dancer at a Lima vu-tavern. They'd wandered from deposit to deposit, the father digging his concessions, the mother signing on at the nearest bordello to pay the rent.

'She only sang, of course,' Jane added. 'Until my father came.' She blew bubbles into her glass. 'So you think I give them what they want at the Casino. By the way, what do you see?'

'I'm afraid I'm your one failure,' I said. 'Nothing. Except you.'

She dropped her eyes. 'That sometimes happens,' she said. 'I'm glad this time.'

A million suns pounded inside me. Until then I'd been reserving judgment on myself.

Harry and Tony were polite, if disappointed.

'I can't believe it,' Harry said sadly. 'I won't. How did you do it?'

'That mystical left-handed approach, of course,' I told him. 'All ancient seas and dark wells.'

'What's she like?' Tony asked eagerly. 'I mean, does she burn or just tingle?'

Jane sang at the Casino every night from eleven to three, but apart from that I suppose we were always together. Sometimes in the late afternoons we'd drive out along the beach to the Scented Desert and sit alone by one of the pools, watching the sun fall away behind the reefs and hills, lulling ourselves on the rose-sick air. When the wind began to blow cool across the sand we'd slip down into the water, bathe ourselves and drive back to town, filling the streets and café terraces with jasmine and musk-rose and helianthemum.

On other evenings we'd go down to one of the quiet bars at Lagoon West, and have supper out on the flats, and Jane would tease the waiters and sing honeybirds and angelcakes to the children who came in across the sand to watch her.

I realize now that I must have achieved a certain notoriety along the beach, but I didn't mind giving the old women – and beside Jane they all seemed to be old women – something to talk about. During the Recess no one cared very much about anything, and for that reason I never questioned myself too closely over my affair with Jane Ciracylides. As I sat on the balcony with her looking out over the cool early evenings or felt her body glowing beside me in the darkness I allowed myself few anxieties.

Absurdly, the only disagreement I ever had with her was over her cheating.

I remember that I once taxed her with it.

'Do you know you've taken over five hundred dollars from me, Jane? You're still doing it. Even now!'

She laughed impishly. 'Do I cheat? I'll let you win one day.'

'But why do you?' I insisted.

'It's more fun to cheat,' she said. 'Otherwise it's so boring.'

'Where will you go when you leave Vermilion Sands?' I asked her.

She looked at me in surprise. 'Why do you say that? I don't think I shall ever leave.'

'Don't tease me, Jane. You're a child of another world than this.'

'My father came from Peru,' she reminded me.

'But you didn't get your voice from him,' I said. 'I wish I could have heard your mother sing. Had she a better voice than yours, Jane?'

'She thought so. My father couldn't stand either of us.'

That was the evening I last saw Jane. We'd changed, and in the half an hour before she left for the Casino we sat on the balcony and I listened to her voice, like a spectral fountain, pour its luminous notes into the air. The music remained with me even after she'd gone, hanging faintly in the darkness around her chair.

I felt curiously sleepy, almost sick on the air she'd left behind, and at 11.30, when I knew she'd be appearing on stage at the Casino, I went out for a walk along the beach.

As I left the elevator I heard music coming from the shop.

At first I thought I'd left one of the audio switches on, but I knew the voice only too well.

The windows of the shop had been shuttered, so I got in through the passage which led from the garage courtyard round at the back of the apartment house.

The lights had been turned out, but a brilliant glow filled the shop, throwing a golden fire on to the tanks along the counters. Across the ceiling liquid colours danced in reflection.

The music I had heard before, but only in overture.

The Arachnid had grown to three times its size. It towered nine feet high out of the shattered lid of the control tank, leaves tumid and inflamed, its calyx as large as a bucket, raging insanely.

Arched forwards into it, her head thrown back, was Jane.

I ran over to her, my eyes filling with light, and grabbed her arm, trying to pull her away from it.

'Jane!' I shouted over the noise. 'Get down!'

She flung my hand away. In her eyes, fleetingly, was a look of shame.

While I was sitting on the stairs in the entrance Tony and Harry drove up.

'Where's Jane?' Harry asked. 'Has anything happened to her? We were down at the Casino.' They both turned towards the music. 'What the hell's going on?'

Tony peered at me suspiciously. 'Steve, anything wrong?'

Harry dropped the bouquet he was carrying and started towards the rear entrance.

'Harry!' I shouted after him. 'Get back!'

Tony held my shoulder. 'Is Jane in there?'

I caught them as they opened the door into the shop.

'Good God!' Harry yelled. 'Let go of me, you fool!' He struggled to get away from me. 'Steve, it's trying to kill her!'

I jammed the door shut and held them back.

I never saw Jane again. The three of us waited in my apartment. When the music died away we went down and found the shop in darkness. The Arachnid had shrunk to its normal size.

The next day it died.

Where Jane went to I don't know. Not long afterwards the Recess ended, and the big government schemes came along and started up all the clocks and kept us too busy working off the lost time to worry about a few bruised petals. Harry told me that Jane had been seen on her way through Red Beach, and I heard recently that someone very like her was doing the nightclubs this side out of Pernambuco.

So if any of you around here keep a choro-florist's, and have a Khan-Arachnid orchid, look out for a golden-skinned woman with insects for eyes. Perhaps she'll play i-Go with you, and I'm sorry to have to say it, but she'll always cheat.

# The Screen Game

Every afternoon during the summer at Ciraquito we play the screen game. After lunch today, when the arcades and café terraces were empty and everyone was lying asleep indoors, three of us drove out in Raymond Mayo's Lincoln along the road to Vermilion Sands.

The season had ended, and already the desert had begun to move in again for the summer, drifting against the yellowing shutters of the cigarette kiosks, surrounding the town with immense banks of luminous ash. Along the horizon the flat-topped mesas rose into the sky like the painted cones of a volcano jungle. The beachhouses had been empty for weeks, and abandoned sand-yachts stood in the centre of the lakes, embalmed in the opaque heat. Only the highway showed any signs of activity, the motion sculpture of concrete ribbon unfolding across the landscape.

Twenty miles from Ciraquito, where the highway forks to Red Beach and Vermilion Sands, we turned on to the remains of an old gravel track that ran away among the sand reefs. Only a year earlier this had been a well-kept private road, but the ornamental gateway lay collapsed to one side, and the guardhouse was a nesting place for scorpions and sand-rays.

Few people ever ventured far up the road. Continuous rock slides disturbed the area, and large sections of the surface had slipped away into the reefs. In addition a curious but unmistakable atmosphere of menace hung over the entire zone, marking it off from the remainder of the desert. The hanging galleries of the reefs were more convoluted and sinister, like the tortured demons of medieval cathedrals. Massive towers of obsidian reared over the roadway like stone gallows, their cornices streaked with iron-red dust. The light seemed duller, unlike the rest of the desert, occasionally flaring into a sepulchral glow as if some subterranean fire-cloud had boiled to the surface of the rocks. The surrounding peaks and spires shut out the desert plain, and the only sounds were the echoes of the engine growling among the hills and the piercing cries of the sand-rays wheeling over the open mouths of the reefs like hieratic birds.

For half a mile we followed the road as it wound like a petrified snake above the reefs, and our conversation became more sporadic and fell away entirely, resuming only when we began our descent through a shallow valley. A few abstract sculptures stood by the roadside. Once these were sonic, responding to the slipstream of a passing car with a series of warning vibratos, but now the Lincoln passed them unrecognized.

Abruptly, around a steep bend, the reefs and peaks vanished, and the wide expanse of an inland sand-lake lay before us, the great summer house of Lagoon West on its shore. Fragments of light haze hung over the dunes like untethered clouds. The tyres cut softly through the cerise sand, and soon we were overrunning what appeared to be the edge of an immense chessboard of black and white marble squares. More statues appeared, some buried to their heads, others toppled from their plinths by the drifting dunes.

Looking out at them this afternoon, I felt, not for the first time, that the whole landscape was compounded of illusion, the hulks of fabulous dreams drifting across it like derelict galleons. As we followed the road towards the lake, the huge wreck of Lagoon West passed us slowly on our left. Its terraces and balconies were deserted. and the once marble-white surface was streaked and lifeless. Staircases ended abruptly in midflight, and the floors hung like sagging marquees.

In the centre of the terrace the screens stood where we had left them the previous afternoon, their zodiacal emblems flashing like serpents. We walked across to them through the hot sunlight. For the next hour we played the screen game, pushing the screens along their intricate pathways, advancing and retreating across the smooth marble floor.

No one watched us, but once, fleetingly, I thought I saw a tall figure in a blue cape hidden in the shadows of a second-floor balcony.

'Emerelda!'

On a sudden impulse I shouted to her, but almost without moving she had vanished among the hibiscus and bougainvillaea. As her name echoed away among the dunes I knew that we had made our last attempt to lure her from the balcony.

'Paul.' Twenty yards away, Raymond and Tony had reached the car. 'Paul, we're leaving.'

Turning my back to them, I looked up at the great bleached hulk of Lagoon West leaning into the sunlight. Somewhere, along the shore of the sand-lake, music was playing faintly, echoing among the exposed quartz veins. A few isolated chords at first, the fragments hung on the afternoon air, the sustained tremolos suspended above my head like the humming of invisible insects.

As the phrases coalesced, I remembered when we had first played the screen game at Lagoon West. I remembered the last tragic battle with the jewelled insects, and I remembered Emerelda Garland...

I first saw Emerelda Garland the previous summer, shortly after the film company arrived in Ciraquito and was invited by Charles Van Stratten to use the locations at Lagoon West. The company, Orpheus Productions, Inc. – known to the aficionados of the café terraces such as Raymond Mayo and Tony Sapphire as the 'ebb tide of the new wave' – was one of those experimental units whose output is destined for a single rapturous showing at the Cannes Film Festival, and who rely for their financial backing on the generosity of the many millionaire dilettantes who apparently feel a compulsive need to cast themselves in the role of Lorenzo de Medici.

Not that there was anything amateurish about the equipment and technical resources of Orpheus Productions. The fleet of location trucks and recording studios which descended on Ciraquito on one of those empty August afternoons looked like the entire D-Day task force, and even the more conservative estimates of the budget for *Aphrodite 80*, the film we helped to make at Lagoon West, amounted to at least twice the gross national product of a Central American republic. What was amateurish was the indifference to normal commercial restraints, and the unswerving dedication to the highest aesthetic standards.

All this, of course, was made possible by the largesse of Charles Van Stratten. To begin with, when we were first coopted into *Aphrodite 80*, some of us were inclined to be amused by Charles's naive attempts to produce a masterpiece, but later we all realized that there was something touching about Charles's earnestness. None of us, however, was aware of the private tragedy which drove him on through the heat and dust of that summer at Lagoon West, and the grim nemesis waiting behind the canvas floats and stage props.

At the time he became the sole owner of Orpheus Productions, Charles Van Stratten had recently celebrated his fortieth birthday, but to all intents he was still a quiet and serious undergraduate. A scion of one of the world's wealthiest banking families, in his early twenties he had twice been briefly married, first to a Neapolitan countess, and then to a Hollywood starlet, but the most influential figure in Charles's life was his mother. This domineering harridan, who sat like an immense ormolu spider in her sombre Edwardian mansion on Park Avenue, surrounded by dark galleries filled with Rubens and Rembrandt, had been widowed shortly after Charles's birth, and obviously regarded Charles as providence's substitute for her husband. Cunningly manipulating a web of trust funds and residuary legacies, she ruthlessly eliminated both Charles's wives (the second committed suicide in a Venetian gondola, the first eloped with his analyst), and then herself died in circumstances of some mystery at the summer-house at Lagoon West.

Despite the immense publicity attached to the Van Stratten family, little was ever known about the old dowager's death – officially she tripped over a second-floor balcony – and Charles retired completely from the limelight of international celebrity for the next five years. Now and then he would emerge briefly at the Venice Biennale, or serve as co-sponsor of some cultural foundation, but otherwise he retreated into the vacuum left by his mother's death. Rumour had it – at least in Ciraquito – that Charles himself had been responsible for her quietus, as if revenging (how long overdue!) the tragedy of Oedipus, when the dowager, scenting the prospect of a third liaison, had descended like Jocasta upon Lagoon West and caught Charles and his paramour *in flagrante*.

Much as I liked the story, the first glimpse of Charles Van Stratten dispelled the possibility. Five years after his mother's death, Charles still behaved as if she were watching his every movement through tripod-mounted opera glasses on some distant balcony. His youthful figure was a little more portly, but his handsome aristocratic face, its strong jaw belied by an indefinable weakness around the mouth, seemed somehow daunted and indecisive, as if he lacked complete conviction in his own identity.

Shortly after the arrival in Ciraquito of Orpheus Productions, the property manager visited the cafés in the artists' quarters, canvassing for scenic designers. Like most of the painters in Ciraquito and Vermilion Sands, I was passing through one of my longer creative pauses. I had stayed on in the town after the season ended, idling away the long, empty afternoons under the awning at the Café Fresco, and was already showing symptoms of beach fatigue – irreversible boredom and inertia. The prospect of actual work seemed almost a novelty.

'*Aphrodite 80*,' Raymond Mayo explained when he returned to our table after a kerb-side discussion. 'The whole thing reeks of integrity – they want local artists to paint the flats, large abstract designs for the desert backgrounds. They'll pay a dollar per square foot.'

'That's rather mean,' I commented.

'The property manager apologized, but Van Stratten is a millionaire – money means nothing to him. If it's any consolation, Raphael and Michelangelo were paid a smaller rate for the Sistine Chapel.'

'Van Stratten has a bigger budget,' Tony Sapphire reminded him. 'Besides, the modern painter is a more complex type, his integrity needs to be buttressed by substantial assurances. Is Paul a painter in the tradition of Leonardo and Larry Rivers, or a cut-price dauber?'

Moodily we watched the distant figure of the property manager move from café to café.

'How many square feet do they want?' I asked.

'About a million,' Raymond said.

Later that afternoon, as we turned off the Red Beach road and were waved on past the guardhouse to Lagoon West, we could hear the sonic sculptures high among the reefs echoing and hooting to the calvacade of cars speeding over the hills. Droves of startled rays scattered in the air like clouds of exploding soot, their frantic cries lost among the spires and reefs. Preoccupied by the prospect of our vast fees – I had hastily sworn in Tony and Raymond as my assistants – we barely noticed the strange landscape we were crossing, the great gargoyles of red basalt that uncoiled themselves into the air like the spires of demented cathedrals. From the Red Beach – Vermilion Sands highway – the hills seemed permanently veiled by the sand haze, and Lagoon West, although given a brief notoriety by the death of Mrs Van Stratten, remained isolated and unknown. From the beach-houses on the southern shore of the sand-lake two miles away, the distant terraces and tiered balconies of the summer-house could just be seen across the fused sand, jutting into the cerise evening sky like a stack of dominoes. There was no access to the house along the beach. Quartz veins cut deep fissures into the surface, the reefs of ragged sandstone reared into the air like the rusting skeletons of forgotten ships.

The whole of Lagoon West was a continuous slide area. Periodically a soft boom would disturb the morning silence as one of the galleries of compacted sand, its intricate grottoes and colonnades like an inverted baroque palace, would suddenly dissolve and avalanche gently into the internal precipice below. Most years Charles Van Stratten was away in Europe, and the house was believed to be empty. The only sound the occupants of the beach villas would hear was the faint music of the sonic sculptures carried across the lake by the thermal rollers.

It was to this landscape, with its imperceptible transition between the real and the superreal, that Charles Van Stratten had brought the camera crews and location vans of Orpheus Productions, Inc. As the Lincoln joined the column of cars moving towards the summer-house, we could see the great canvas hoardings, at least two hundred yards wide and thirty feet high, which a team of construction workers was erecting among the reefs a quarter of a mile from the house. Decorated with abstract symbols, these would serve as backdrops to the action, and form a fragmentary labyrinth winding in and out of the hills and dunes.

One of the large terraces below the summer-house served as a parking lot, and we made our way through the unloading crews to where a group of men in crocodile-skin slacks and raffia shirts – then the uniform of avant-garde film men – were gathered around a heavily jowled man like a perspiring bear who was holding a stack of script boards under one arm and gesticulating wildly with the other. This was Orson Kanin, director of *Aphrodite 80* and co-owner with Charles Van Stratten of Orpheus Productions. Sometime *enfant terrible* of the futurist cinema, but now a portly barrel-stomached fifty, Kanin had made his reputation some twenty years earlier with *Blind Orpheus*, a neo-Freudian, horror-film version of the Greek legend. According to Kanin's interpretation, Orpheus deliberately breaks the taboo and looks Eurydice in the face because he wants to be rid of her; in a famous nightmare sequence which projects his unconscious loathing, he becomes increasingly aware of something cold and strange about his resurrected wife, and finds that she is a disintegrating corpse.

As we joined the periphery of the group, a characteristic Kanin script conference was in full swing, a non-stop pantomime of dramatized incidents from the imaginary script, anecdotes, salary promises and bad puns, all delivered in a rich fruity baritone. Sitting on the balustrade beside Kanin was a handsome, youthful man with a sensitive face whom I recognized to be Charles Van Stratten. Now and then, *sotto voce*, he would interject some comment that would be noted by one of the secretaries and incorporated into Kanin's monologue.

As the conference proceeded I gathered that they would begin to shoot the film in some three weeks' time, and that it would be performed entirely without script. Kanin only seemed perturbed by the fact that no one had yet been found to play the Aphrodite of *Aphrodite 80* but Charles Van Stratten interposed here to assure Kanin that he himself would provide the actress.

At this eyebrows were raised knowingly. 'Of course,' Raymond murmured. '*Droit de seigneur*. I wonder who the next Mrs Van Stratten is?'

But Charles Van Stratten seemed unaware of these snide

undertones. Catching sight of me, he excused himself and came over to us.

'Paul Golding?' He took my hand in a soft but warm grip. We had never met but I presumed he recognized me from the photographs in the art reviews. 'Kanin told me you'd agreed to do the scenery. It's wonderfully encouraging.' He spoke in a light, pleasant voice absolutely without affectation. 'There's so much confusion here it's a relief to know that at least the scenic designs will be first-class.' Before I could demur he took my arm and began to walk away along the terrace towards the hoardings in the distance. 'Let's get some air. Kanin will keep this up for a couple of hours at least.'

Leaving Raymond and Tony, I followed him across the huge marble squares.

'Kanin keeps worrying about his leading actress,' he went on. 'Kanin always marries his latest protégé – he claims it's the only way he can make them respond fully to his direction, but I suspect there's an old-fashioned puritan lurking within the cavalier. This time he's going to be disappointed, though not by the actress, may I add. The Aphrodite I have in mind will outshine Milos's.'

'The film sounds rather ambitious,' I commented, 'but I'm sure Kanin is equal to it.'

'Of course he is. He's very nearly a genius, and that should be good enough.' He paused for a moment, hands in the pockets of his dove-grey suit, before translating himself like a chess piece along a diagonal square. 'It's a fascinating subject, you know. The title is misleading, a box-office concession. The film is really Kanin's final examination of the Orpheus legend. The whole question of the illusions which exist in any relationship to make it workable, and of the barriers we willingly accept to hide ourselves from each other. How much reality can we stand?'

We reached one of the huge hoardings that stretched away among the reefs. Jutting upwards from the spires and grottoes, it seemed to shut off half the sky, and already I felt the atmosphere of shifting illusion and reality that enclosed the whole of Lagoon West, the subtle displacement of time and space. The great hoardings seemed to be both barriers and corridors. Leading away radially from the house and breaking up the landscape, of which they revealed sudden unrelated glimpses, they introduced a curiously appealing element of uncertainty into the placid afternoon, an impression reinforced by the emptiness and enigmatic presence of the summer-house.

Returning to Kanin's conference, we followed the edge of the terrace. Here the sand had drifted over the balustrade which divided the public sector of the grounds from the private. Looking up at the lines of balconies on the south face, I noticed someone standing in the shadows below one of the awnings.

Something flickered brightly from the ground at my feet. Momentarily reflecting the full disc of the sun, like a polished node of sapphire or quartz, the light flashed among the dust, then seemed to dart sideways below the balustrade.

'My God, a scorpion!' I pointed to the insect crouching away from us, the red scythe of its tail beckoning slowly. I assumed that the thickened chitin of the headpiece was reflecting the light, and then saw that a small faceted stone had been set into the skull. As it edged forward into the light, the jewel burned in the sun like an incandescent crystal.

Charles Van Stratten stepped past me. Almost pushing me aside, he glanced towards the shuttered balconies. He feinted deftly with one foot at the scorpion, and before the insect could recover had stamped it into the dust.

'Right, Paul,' he said in a firm voice. 'I think your suggested designs are excellent. You've caught the spirit of the whole thing exactly, as I knew you would.' Buttoning his jacket he made off towards the film unit, barely pausing to scrape the damp husk of the crushed carapace from his shoe.

I caught up with him. 'That scorpion was jewelled,' I said. 'There was a diamond, or zircon, inset in the head.'

He waved impatiently and then took a pair of large sunglasses from his breast pocket. Masked, his face seemed harder and more autocratic, reminding me of our true relationship.

'An illusion, Paul,' he said. 'Some of the insects here are dangerous. You must be more careful.' His point made, he relaxed and flashed me his most winning smile.

Rejoining Tony and Raymond, I watched Charles Van Stratten walk off through the technicians and stores staff. His stride was noticeably more purposive, and he brushed aside an assistant producer without bothering to turn his head.

'Well, Paul.' Raymond greeted me expansively. 'There's no script, no star, no film in the cameras, and no one has the faintest idea what he's supposed to be doing. But there are a million square feet of murals waiting to be painted. It all seems perfectly straightforward.'

I looked back across the terrace to where we had seen the scorpion. 'I suppose it is,' I said.

Somewhere in the dust a jewel glittered brightly.

Two days later I saw another of the jewelled insects.

Suppressing my doubts about Charles Van Stratten, I was busy preparing my designs for the hoardings. Although Raymond's first estimate of a million square feet was exaggerated – less than a tenth of this would be needed – the amount of work and materials required was substantial. In effect I was about to do nothing less than repaint the entire desert.

Each morning I went out to Lagoon West and worked among the reefs, adapting the designs to the contours and colours of the terrain. Most of the time I was alone in the hot sun. After the initial frenzy of activity Orpheus Productions had lost momentum. Kanin had gone off to a film festival at Red Beach and most of the assistant producers and writers had retired to the swimming pool at the Hotel Neptune in Vermilion Sands. Those who remained behind at Lagoon West were now sitting half asleep under the coloured umbrellas erected around the mobile cocktail bar.

The only sign of movement came from Charles Van Stratten, roving tirelessly in his white suit among the reefs and sand spires. Now and then I would hear one of the sonic sculptures on the upper balconies of the summer-house change its note, and turn to see him standing beside it. His sonic profile evoked a strange, soft sequence of chords, interwoven by sharper, almost plaintive notes that drifted away across the still afternoon air towards the labyrinth of great hoardings that now surrounded the summer-house. All day he would wander among them, pacing out the perimeters and diagonals as if trying to square the circle of some private enigma, the director of a Wagnerian psychodrama that would involve us all in its cathartic unfolding.

Shortly after noon, when an intense pall of yellow light lay over the desert, dissolving the colours in its glazed mantle, I sat down on the balustrade, waiting for the meridian to pass. The sand-lake shimmered in the thermal gradients like an immense pool of sluggish wax. A few yards away something flickered in the bright sand, a familiar flare of light. Shielding my eyes, I found the source, the diminutive Promethean bearer of this brilliant corona. The spider, a Black Widow, approached on its stilted legs, a blaze of staccato signals pouring from its crown. It stopped and pivoted, revealing the large sapphire inset into its head.

More points of light flickered. Within a moment the entire terrace sparkled with jewelled light. Quickly I counted a score of the insects – turquoised scorpions, a purple mantis with a giant topaz like a tiered crown, and more than a dozen spiders, pinpoints of emerald and sapphire light lancing from their heads.

Above them, hidden in the shadows among the bougainvillaea on her balcony, a tall white-faced figure in a blue gown looked down at me.

I stepped over the balustrade, carefully avoiding the motionless insects. Separated from the remainder of the terrace by the west wing of the summer-house, I had entered a new zone, where the bonelike pillars of the loggia, the glimmering surface of the sand-lake, and the jewelled insects enclosed me in a sudden empty limbo.

For a few moments I stood below the balcony from which the insects had emerged, still watched by this strange sybilline figure presiding over her private world. I felt that I had strayed across the margins of a dream, on to an internal landscape of the psyche projected upon the sun-filled terraces around me.

But before I could call to her, footsteps grated softly in the loggia. A dark-haired man of about fifty, with a closed, expressionless face, stood among the columns, his black suit neatly buttoned. He looked down at me with the impassive eyes of a funeral director.

The shutters withdrew upon the balcony, and the jewelled insects returned from their foray. Surrounding me, their brilliant crowns glittered with diamond hardness.

Each afternoon, as I returned from the reefs with my sketch pad, I would see the jewelled insects moving in the sunlight beside the lake, while their blue-robed mistress, the haunted Venus of Lagoon West, watched them from her balcony. Despite the frequency of her appearances, Charles Van Stratten made no attempt to explain her presence. His elaborate preparations for the filming of *Aphrodite 80* almost complete, he became more and more preoccupied.

An outline scenario had been agreed on. To my surprise the first scene was to be played on the lake terrace, and would take the form of a shadow ballet, for which I painted a series of screens to be moved about like chess pieces. Each was about twelve feet high, a large canvas mounted on a wooden trestle, representing one of the zodiac signs. Like the protagonist of *The Cabinet of Dr Caligari*, trapped in a labyrinth of tilting walls, the Orphic hero of *Aphrodite 80* would appear searching for his lost Eurydice among the shifting time stations.

So the screen game, which we were to play tirelessly on so many occasions, made its appearance. As I completed the last of the screens and watched a group of extras perform the first movements of the game under Charles Van Stratten's directions, I began to realize the extent to which we were all supporting players in a gigantic charade of Charles's devising.

Its real object soon became apparent.

The summer house was deserted when I drove out to Lagoon West the next weekend, an immense canopy of silence hanging over the lake and the surrounding hills. The twelve screens stood on the terrace above the beach, their vivid, heraldic designs melting into blurred pools of turquoise and carmine which bled away in horizontal layers across the air. Someone had rearranged the screens to form a narrow spiral corridor. As I straightened them, the train of a white gown disappeared with a startled flourish among the shadows within.

Guessing the probable identity of this pale and nervous intruder, I stepped quietly into the corridor. I pushed back one of the screens, a large Scorpio in royal purple, and suddenly found myself in the centre of the maze, little more than an arm's length from the strange figure I had seen on the balcony. For a moment she failed to notice me. Her exquisite white face, like a marble mask, veined by a faint shadow of violet that seemed like a delicate interior rosework, was raised to the canopy of sunlight which cut across the upper edges of the screens. She wore a long beach-robe, with a flared hood that enclosed her head like a protective bower.

One of the jewelled insects nestled on a fold above her neck. There was a curious glacé immobility about her face, investing the white skin with an almost sepulchral quality, the soft down which covered it like grave's dust.

'Who –?' Startled, she stepped back. The insects scattered at her feet, winking on the floor like a jewelled carpet. She stared at me in surprise, drawing the hood of her gown around her face like an exotic flower withdrawing into its foliage. Conscious of the protective circle of insects, she lifted her chin and composed herself.

'I'm sorry to interrupt you,' I said. 'I didn't realize there was anyone here. I'm flattered that you like the screens.'

The autocratic chin lowered fractionally, and her head, with its swirl of blue hair, emerged from the hood. '*You* painted these?' she confirmed. 'I thought they were Dr Gruber's ...' She broke off, tired or bored by the effort of translating her thoughts into speech.

'They're for Charles Van Stratten's film,' I explained. '*Aphrodite 80*. The film about Orpheus he's making here.' I added: 'You must ask him to give you a part. You'd be a great adornment.'

'A film?' Her voice cut across mine. 'Listen. Are you sure they are for this film? It's important that I know –'

'Quite sure.' Already I was beginning to find her exhausting. Talking to her was like walking across a floor composed of blocks of varying heights, an analogy reinforced by the squares of the terrace, into which her presence had let another random dimension. 'They're going to film one of the scenes here. Of course,' I volunteered when she greeted this news with a frown, 'you're free to play with the screens. In fact, if you like, I'll paint some for you.'

'Will you?' From the speed of the response I could see that I had at last penetrated to the centre of her attention. 'Can you start today? Paint as many as you can, just like these. Don't change the designs.' She gazed around at the zodiacal symbols looming from the shadows like the murals painted in dust and blood on the walls of a Toltec funeral corridor. 'They're wonderfully alive, sometimes I think they're even more real that Dr Gruber. Though –' here she faltered '– I don't know how I'll pay you. You see, they don't give me any money.' She smiled at me like an anxious child, then brightened suddenly. She knelt down and picked one of the jewelled scorpions from the floor. 'Would you like one of these?' The flickering insect, with its brilliant ruby crown, tottered unsteadily on her white palm.

Footsteps approached, the firm rap of leather on marble. 'They may be rehearsing today,' I said. 'Why don't you watch? I'll take you on a tour of the sets.'

As I started to pull back the screens I felt the long fingers of her hand on my arm. A mood of acute agitation had come over her.

'Relax,' I said. 'I'll tell them to go away. Don't worry, they won't spoil your game.'

'No! Listen, please!' The insects scattered and darted as the outer circle of screens was pulled back. In a few seconds the whole world of illusion was dismantled and exposed to the hot sunlight.

Behind the Scorpio appeared the watchful face of the dark-suited man. A smile played like a snake on his lips.

'Ah, Miss Emerelda,' he greeted her in a purring voice. 'I think you should come indoors. The afternoon heat is intense and you tire very easily.'

The insects retreated from his black patent shoes. Looking into his eyes, I caught a glimpse of deep reserves of patience, like that of an experienced nurse used to the fractious moods and uncertainties of a chronic invalid.

'Not now,' Emerelda insisted. 'I'll come in a few moments.'

'I've just been describing the screens,' I explained.

'So I gather, Mr Golding,' he rejoined evenly. 'Miss Emerelda,' he called.

For a moment they appeared to have reached deadlock. Emerelda, the jewelled insects at her feet, stood beside me, her hand on my arm, while her guardian waited, the same thin smile on his lips. More footsteps approached. The remaining screens were pushed back and the plump, well-talcumed figure of Charles Van Stratten appeared, his urbane voice raised in greeting.

'What's this – a story conference?' he asked jocularly. He broke off when he saw Emerelda and her guardian. 'Dr Gruber? What's going – Emerelda my dear?'

Smoothly, Dr Gruber interjected. 'Good afternoon, sir. Miss Garland is about to return to her room.'

'Good, good,' Charles exclaimed. For the first time I had known him he seemed unsure of himself. He made a tentative approach to Emerelda, who was staring at him fixedly. She drew her robe around her and stepped quickly through the screens. Charles moved forwards, uncertain whether to follow her.

'Thank you, doctor,' he muttered. There was a flash of patent leather heels, and Charles and I were alone among the screens. On the floor at our feet was a single jewelled mantis. Without thinking, Charles bent down to pick it up, but the insect snapped at him. He withdrew his fingers with a wan smile, as if accepting the finality of Emerelda's departure.

Recognizing me with an effort, Charles pulled himself together. 'Well, Paul, I'm glad you and Emerelda were getting on so well. I knew you'd make an excellent job of the screens.'

We walked out into the sunlight. After a pause he said, 'That is Emerelda Garland; she's lived here since mother died. It was a tragic experience, Dr Gruber thinks she may never recover.'

'He's her doctor?'

Charles nodded. 'One of the best I could find. For some reason Emerelda feels herself responsible for mother's death. She's refused to leave here.'

I pointed to the screens. 'Do you think they help?'

'Of course. Why do you suppose we're here at all?' He lowered his voice, although Lagoon West was deserted. 'Don't tell Kanin yet, but you've just met the star of *Aphrodite 80*.'

'What?' Incredulously, I stopped. 'Emerelda? Do you mean that she's going to play –?'

'Eurydice.' Charles nodded. 'Who better?'

'But Charles, she's ...' I searched for a discreet term.

'That's exactly the point. Believe me, Paul,' – here Charles smiled at me with an expression of surprising canniness – 'this film is not as abstract as Kanin thinks. In fact, its sole purpose is therapeutic. You see, Emerelda was once a minor film actress, I'm convinced the camera crews and sets will help to carry her back to the past, to the period before her appalling shock. It's the only way left, a sort of total psychodrama. The choice of theme, the Orpheus legend and its associations, fit the situation exactly – I see myself as a latter-day Orpheus trying to rescue my Eurydice from Dr Gruber's hell.' He smiled bleakly, as if aware of the slenderness of the analogy and its faint hopes. 'Emerelda's withdrawn completely into her private world, spends all her time inlaying these insects with her jewels. With luck the screens will lead her out into the rest of this synthetic landscape. After all, if she knows that everything around her is unreal she'll cease to fear it.'

'But can't you simply move her physically from Lagoon West?' I asked. 'Perhaps Gruber is the wrong doctor for her. I can't understand why you've kept her here all these years.'

'I haven't kept her, Paul,' he said earnestly. 'She's clung to this place and its nightmare memories. Now she even refuses to let me come near her.'

We parted and he walked away among the deserted dunes. In the background the great hoardings I had designed shut out the distant reefs and mesas. Huge blocks of colour had been sprayed on to the designs, superimposing a new landscape upon the desert. The geometric forms loomed and wavered in the haze, like the shifting symbols of a beckoning dream.

As I watched Charles disappear, I felt a sudden sense of pity for his subtle but naive determination. Wondering whether to warn him of his almost certain failure, I rubbed the raw bruises on my arm. While she started at him, Emerelda's fingers had clasped my arm with unmistakable fierceness, her sharp nails locked together like a clamp of daggers.

So, each afternoon, we began to play the screen game, moving the zodiacal emblems to and fro across the terrace. As I sat on the balustrade and watched Emerelda Garland's first tentative approaches, I wondered how far all of us were becoming ensnared by Charles Van Stratten, by the painted desert and the sculpture singing from the aerial terraces of the summer-house. Into all this Emerelda Garland had now emerged, like a beautiful but nervous wraith. First she would slip among the screens as they gathered below her balcony, and then, hidden behind the large Virgo at their centre, would move across the floor towards the lake, enclosed by the shifting pattern of screens.

Once I left my seat beside Charles and joined the game. Gradually I manœuvred my screen, a small Sagittarius, into the centre of the maze where I found Emerelda in a narrow shifting cubicle, swaying from side to side as if entranced by the rhythm of the game, the insects scattered at her feet. When I approached she clasped my hand and ran away down a corridor, her gown falling loosely around her bare shoulders. As the screens once more reached the summer-house, she gathered her train in one hand and disappeared among the columns of the loggia.

Walking back to Charles, I found a jewelled mantis nestling like a brooch on the lapel of my jacket, its crown of amethyst melting in the fading sunlight.

'She's coming out, Paul,' Charles said. 'Already she's accepted the screens, soon she'll be able to leave them.' He frowned at the jewelled mantis on my palm. 'A present from Emerelda. Rather two-edged, I think, those stings are dangerous. Still, she's grateful to you, Paul, as I am. Now I know that only the artist can create an absolute reality. Perhaps you should paint a few more screens.'

'Gladly, Charles, if you're sure that . . .'

But Charles merely nodded to himself and walked away towards the film crew.

During the next days I painted several new screens, duplicating the zodiacal emblems, so that each afternoon the game became progressively slower and more intricate, the thirty screens forming a multiple labyrinth. For a few minutes, at the climax of the game, I would find Emerelda in the dark centre with the screens jostling and tilting around her, the sculpture on the roof hooting in the narrow interval of open sky.

'Why don't you join the game?' I asked Charles. After his earlier elation he was becoming impatient. Each evening as he drove back to Ciraquito the plume of dust behind his speeding Maserati would rise progressively higher into the pale air. He had lost interest in *Aphrodite 80*. Fortunately Kanin had found that the painted desert of Lagoon West could not be reproduced by any existing colour process, and the film was now being shot from models in a rented studio at Red Beach. 'Perhaps if Emerelda saw you in the maze . . .'

'No, no.' Charles shook his head categorically, then stood up and paced about. 'Paul, I'm less sure of this now.'

Unknown to him, I had painted a dozen more screens. Early that morning I had hidden them among the others on the terrace.

Three nights later, tired of conducting my courtship of Emerelda Garland within a painted maze, I drove out to Lagoon West, climbing through the darkened hills whose contorted forms reared in the swinging headlamps like the smoke clouds of some sunken hell. In the distance, beside the lake, the angular terraces of the summer-house hung in the grey opaque air, as if suspended by invisible wires from the indigo clouds which stretched like velvet towards the few faint lights along the beach two miles away.

The sculptures on the upper balconies were almost silent, and I moved past them carefully, drawing only a few muted chords from them, the faint sounds carried from one statue to the next to the roof of the summer-house and then lost on the midnight air.

From the loggia I looked down at the labyrinth of screens, and at the jewelled insects scattered across the terrace, sparkling on the dark marble like the reflection of a star field.

I found Emerelda Garland among the screens, her white face an oval halo in the shadows, almost naked in a silk gown like a veil of moonlight. She was leaning against a huge Taurus with her pale arms outstretched at her sides, like Europa supplicant before the bull, the luminous spectres of the zodiac guard surrounding her. Without moving her head, she watched me approach and take her hands. Her blue hair swirled in the dark wind as we moved through the screens and crossed the staircase into the summer-house. The expression on her face, whose porcelain planes reflected the torquoise light of her eyes, was one of almost terrifying calm, as if she were moving through some inner dreamscape of the psyche with the confidence of a sleepwalker. My arm around her waist, I guided her up the steps to her suite, realizing that I was less her lover than the architect of her fantasies. For a moment the ambiguous nature of my role, and the questionable morality of abducting a beautiful but insane woman, made me hesitate.

We had reached the inner balcony which ringed the central hall of the summer-house. Below us a large sonic-sculpture emitted a tense nervous pulse, as if roused from its midnight silence by my hesitant step.

'Wait!' I pulled Emerelda back from the next flight of stairs, rousing her from her self-hypnotic torpor. 'Up there!'

A silent figure in a dark suit stood at the rail outside the door of Emerelda's suite, the downward inclination of his head clearly perceptible.

'Oh, my God!' With both hands Emerelda clung tightly to my arm, her smooth face seized by a rictus of horror and anticipation. 'She's there ... for heaven's sake, Paul, take me–'

'It's Gruber!' I snapped. 'Dr Gruber! Emerelda!'

As we recrossed the entrance the train of Emerelda's gown drew a discordant wail from the statue. In the moonlight the insects still flickered like a carpet of diamonds. I held her shoulders, trying to revive her.

'Emerelda! We'll leave here – take you away from Lagoon West and this insane place.' I pointed to my car, parked by the beach among the dunes. 'We'll go to Vermilion Sands or Red Beach, you'll be able to forget Dr Gruber for ever.'

We hurried towards the car, Emerelda's gown gathering up the insects as we swept past them. I heard her short cry in the moonlight and she tore away from me. I stumbled among the flickering insects. From my knees I saw her disappear into the screens.

For the next ten minutes, as I watched from the darkness by the beach, the jewelled insects moved towards her across the terrace, their last light fading like a vanishing night river.

I walked back to my car, and a quiet, white-suited figure appeared among the dunes and waited for me in the cool amber air, hands deep in his jacket pockets.

'You're a better painter than you know,' Charles said when I took my seat behind the wheel. 'On the last two nights she has made the same escape from me.'

He stared reflectively from the window as we drove back to

Ciraquito, the sculptures in the canyon keening behind us like banshees.

The next afternoon, as I guessed, Charles Van Stratten at last played the screen game. He arrived shortly after the game had begun, walking through the throng of extras and cameramen near the car park, hands still thrust deep into the pockets of his white suit as if his sudden appearance among the dunes the previous night and his present arrival were continuous in time. He stopped by the balustrade on the opposite side of the terrace, where I sat with Tony Sapphire and Raymond Mayo, and stared pensively at the slow shuttling movements of the game, his grey eyes hidden below their blond brows.

By now there were so many screens in the game – over forty (I had secretly added more in an attempt to save Emerelda) – that most of the movement was confined to the centre of the group, as if emphasizing the self-immolated nature of the ritual. What had begun as a pleasant divertimento, a picturesque introduction to *Aphrodite 80*, had degenerated into a macabre charade, transforming the terrace into the exercise area of a nightmare.

Discouraged or bored by the slowness of the game, one by one the extras taking part began to drop out, sitting down on the balustrade beside Charles. Eventually only Emerelda was left – in my mind I could see her gliding in and out of the nexus of corridors, protected by the zodiacal deities I had painted – and now and then one of the screens in the centre would tilt slightly.

'You've designed a wonderful trap for her, Paul,' Raymond Mayo mused. 'A cardboard asylum.'

'It was Van Stratten's suggestion. We thought they might help her.'

Somewhere, down by the beach, a sculpture had begun to play, and its plaintive voice echoed over our heads. Several of the older sculptures whose sonic cores had corroded had been broken up and left on the beach, where they had taken root again. When the heat gradients roused them to life they would emit a brief strangled music, fractured parodies of their former song.

'Paul!' Tony Sapphire pointed across the terrace. 'What's going on? There's something —'

Fifty yards from us, Charles Van Stratten had stepped over the balustrade, and now stood out on one of the black marble squares, hands loosely at his sides, like a single chess piece opposing the massed array of the screens. Everyone else had gone, and the three of us were now alone with Charles and the hidden occupant of the screens.

The harsh song of the rogue sculpture still pierced the air. Two miles away, through the haze which partly obscured the distant shore, the beach-houses jutted among the dunes, and the fused surface of the lake, in which so many objects were embedded, seams of jade and obsidian, was like a segment of embalmed time, from which the music of the sculpture was a slowly expiring leak. The heat over the vermilion surface was like molten quartz, stirring sluggishly to reveal the distant mesas and reefs.

The haze cleared and the spires of the sand reefs seemed to loom forward, their red barbs clawing towards us through the air. The light drove through the opaque surface of the lake, illuminating its fossilized veins, and the threnody of the dying sculpture lifted to a climax.

'Emerelda!'

As we stood up, roused by his shout, Charles Van Stratten was running across the terrace. 'Emerelda!'

Before we could move he began to pull back the screens. toppling them backwards on to the ground. Within a few moments the terrace was a mêlée of tearing canvas and collapsing trestles, the huge emblems flung left and right out of his path like disintegrating floats at the end of a carnival.

Only when the original nucleus of half a dozen screens was left did he pause, hands on hips.

'Emerelda!' he shouted thickly.

Raymond turned to me. 'Paul, stop him, for heaven's sake!'

Striding forward, Charles pulled back the last of the screens. We had a sudden glimpse of Emerelda Garland retreating from the inrush of sunlight, her white gown flared around her like the broken wings of some enormous bird. Then, with an explosive flash, a brilliant vortex of light erupted from the floor at Emerelda's feet, a cloud of jewelled spiders and scorpions rose through the air and engulfed Charles Van Stratten.

Hands raised helplessly to shield his head, he raced across the terrace, the armada of jewelled insects pursuing him, spinning and diving on to his head. Just before he disappeared among the dunes by the beach, we saw him for a last terrifying moment, clawing helplessly at the jewelled helmet stitched into his face and shoulders. His voice rang out, a sustained cry on the note of the dying sculptures, lost on the stinging flight of the insects.

We found him among the sculptures, face downwards in the hot sand, the fabric of his white suit lacerated by a hundred punctures. Around him were scattered the jewels and crushed bodies of the insects he had killed, their knotted legs and mandibles like abstract ideograms, the sapphires and zircons dissolving in the light.

His swollen hands were filled with the jewels. The cloud of insects returned to the summer-house, where Dr Gruber's black-suited figure was silhouetted against the sky, poised on the white ledge like some minatory bird of nightmare. The only sounds came from the sculptures, which had picked up Charles Van Stratten's last cry and incorporated it into their own self-requiem.

'... *"She ... killed"* ...' Raymond stopped, shaking his head in amazement. 'Paul, can you hear them, the words are unmistakable.'

Stepping through the metal barbs of the sculpture, I knelt beside Charles, watching as one of the jewelled scorpions crawled from below his chin and scuttled away across the sand.

'Not him,' I said. 'What he was shouting was *"She killed – Mrs Van Stratten."* The old dowager, his mother. That's the real clue to this fantastic menage. Last night, when we saw Gruber by the rail outside her room – I realize now that was where the old harridan was standing when Emerelda pushed her. For years Charles kept her alone with her guilt here, probably afraid that he might be incriminated if the truth emerged – perhaps he was more responsible than we imagine. What he failed to realize was that Emerelda had lived so long with her guilt that she'd confused it with the person of Charles himself. Killing him was her only release –'

I broke off to find that Raymond and Tony had gone and were already half way back to the terrace. There was the distant sound of raised voices as members of the film company approached, and whistles shrilled above the exhaust of cars.

The bulky figure of Kanin came through the dunes, flanked by a trio of assistant producers. Their incredulous faces gaped at the prostrate body. The voices of the sulptures faded for the last time, carrying with them into the depths of the fossil lake the final plaintive cry of Charles Van Stratten.

A year later, after Orpheus Productions had left Lagoon West and the scandal surrounding Charles's death had subsided, we drove out again to the summer-house. It was one of those dull featureless afternoons when the desert is without lustre, the distant hills illuminated by brief flashes of light, and the great summer-house seemed drab and lifeless. The servants and Dr Gruber had left, and the estate was beginning to run down. Sand covered long stretches of the roadway, and the dunes rolled across the open terraces, toppling the sculptures. These were silent now, and the sepulchral emptiness was only broken by the hidden presence of Emerelda Garland.

We found the screens where they had been left, and on an impulse spent the first afternoon digging them out of the sand. Those that had rotted in the sunlight we burned in a pyre on the beach, and perhaps the ascending plumes of purple and carmine smoke first brought our presence to Emerelda. The next afternoon, as we played the screen game, I was conscious of her watching us, and saw a gleam of her blue gown among the shadows.

However, although we played each afternoon throughout the summer, she never joined us, despite the new screens I painted and added to the group. Only on the night I visited Lagoon West alone did she come down, but I could hear the voices of the sculptures calling again and fled at the sight of her white face.

By some acoustic freak, the dead sculptures along the beach had revived themselves, and once again I heard the faint haunted echoes of Charles Van Stratten's last cry before he was killed by the jewelled insects. All over the deserted summer-house the low refrain was taken up by the statues, echoing through the empty galleries and across the moonlit terraces, carried away to the mouths of the sand reefs, the last dark music of the painted night.

# The Singing Statues

Again last night, as the dusk air began to move across the desert from Lagoon West, I heard fragments of music coming in on the thermal rollers, remote and fleeting, echoes of the love-song of Lunora Goalen. Walking out over the copper sand to the reefs where the sonic sculptures grow, I wandered through the darkness among the metal gardens, searching for Lunora's voice. No one tends the sculptures now and most of them have gone to seed, but on an impulse I cut away a helix and carried it back to my villa, planting it in the quartz bed below the balcony. All night it sang to me, telling me of Lunora and the strange music she played to herself...

It must be just over three years ago that I first saw Lunora Goalen, in Georg Nevers's gallery on Beach Drive. Every summer at the height of the season at Vermilion Sands, Georg staged a special exhibition of sonic sculpture for the tourists. Shortly after we opened one morning I was sitting inside my large statue, *Zero Orbit*, plugging in the stereo amplifiers, when Georg suddenly gasped into the skin mike and a boom like a thunderclap nearly deafened me.

Head ringing like a gong, I climbed out of the sculpture, ready to crown Georg with a nearby maquette. Putting an elegant fingertip to his lips, he gave me that look which between artist and dealer signals one thing: *Rich client.*

The sculptures in the gallery entrance had begun to hum as someone came in, but the sunlight reflected off the bonnet of a white Rolls-Royce outside obscured the doorway.

Then I saw her, hovering over the stand of art journals, followed by her secretary, a tall purse-mouthed Frenchwoman almost as famous from the newsmagazines as her mistress.

Lunora Goalen, I thought, can *all* our dreams come true? She wore an ice-cool sliver of blue silk that shimmered as she moved towards the first statue, a toque hat of black violets and bulky dark glasses that hid her face and were a nightmare to cameramen. While she paused by the statue, one of Arch Penko's frenetic tangles that looked like a rimless bicycle wheel, listening to its arms vibrate and howl, Nevers and I involuntarily steadied ourselves against the wing-piece of my sculpture.

In general it's probably true that the most maligned species on Earth is the wealthy patron of modern art. Laughed at by the public, exploited by dealers, even the artists regard them simply as meal tickets. Lunora Goalen's superb collection of sonic sculpture on the roof of her Venice palazzo, and the million dollars' worth of generous purchases spread around her apartments in Paris, London and New York, represented freedom and life to a score of sculptors, but few felt any gratitude towards Miss Goalen.

Nevers was hesitating, apparently suffering from a sudden intention tremor, so I nudged his elbow.

'Come on,' I murmured. 'This is the apocalypse. Let's go.'

Nevers turned on me icily, noticing, apparently for the first time, my rust-stained slacks and three-day stubble.

'Milton!' he snapped. 'For God's sake, vanish! Sneak out through the freight exit.' He jerked his head at my sculpture. 'And switch that insane thing off! How did I ever let it in here?'

Lunora's secretary, Mme Charcot, spotted us at the rear of the gallery. Georg shot out four inches of immaculate cuff and swayed forward, the smile on his face as wide as a bulldozer. I backed away behind my sculpture, with no intention of leaving and letting Nevers cut my price just for the cachet of making a sale to Lunora Goalen.

Georg was bowing all over the gallery, oblivious of Mme Charcot's contemptuous sneer. He led Lunora over to one of the exhibits and fumbled with the control panel, selecting the alto lift which would resonate most flatteringly with her own body tones. Unfortunately the statue was Sigismund Lubitsch's *Big End*, a squat bull-necked drum like an enormous toad that at its sweetest emitted a rasping grunt. An old-style railroad tycoon might have elicited a sympathetic chord from it, but its response to Lunora was like a bull's to a butterfly.

They moved on to another sculpture, and Mme Charcot gestured to the white-gloved chauffeur standing by the Rolls. He climbed in and moved the car down the street, taking with it the beach crowds beginning to gather outside the gallery. Able now to see Lunora clearly against the hard white walls, I stepped into *Orbit* and watched her closely through the helixes.

Of course I already knew everything about Lunora Goalen. A thousand magazine exposés had catalogued *ad nauseam* her strange flawed beauty, her fits of melancholy and compulsive roving around the world's capitals. Her brief career as a film actress had faltered at first, less as a consequence of her modest, though always interesting, talents than of her simple failure to register photogenically. By a macabre twist of fate, after a major car accident had severely injured her face she had become an extraordinary success. That strangely marred profile and nervous gaze had filled cinemas from Paris to Pernambuco. Unable to bear this tribute to her plastic surgeons, Lunora had abruptly abandoned her career and become a leading patron of the fine arts. Like Garbo in the '40s and '50s, she flitted elusively through the gossip columns and society pages in unending flight from herself.

Her face was the clue. As she took off her sunglasses I could see the curious shadow that fell across it, numbing the smooth white skin. There was a dead glaze in her slate-blue eyes, an uneasy tension around the mouth. Altogether I had a vague impression of something unhealthy, of a Venus with a secret vice.

Nevers was switching on sculptures right and left like a lunatic magician, and the noise was a babel of competing senso-cells, some of the statues responding to Lunora's enigmatic presence, others to Nevers and the secretary.

Lunora shook her head slowly, mouth hardening as the noise irritated her. 'Yes, Mr Nevers,' she said in her slightly husky voice, 'it's all very clever, but a bit of a headache. I *live* with my sculpture, I want something intimate and personal.'

'Of course, Miss Goalen,' Nevers agreed hurriedly, looking around desperately. As he knew only too well, sonic sculpture was now nearing the apogee of its abstract phase; twelve-tone blips and zooms were all that most statues emitted. No purely representational sound, responding to Lunora, for example, with a Mozart rondo or (better) a Webern quartet, had been built for ten years. I guessed that her early purchases were wearing out and that she was hunting the cheaper galleries in tourist haunts like Vermilion Sands in the hope of finding something designed for middle-brow consumption.

Lunora looked up pensively at *Zero Orbit*, towering at the rear of the gallery next to Nevers's desk, apparently unaware that I was hiding inside it. Suddenly realizing that the possibility of selling the statue had miraculously arisen, I crouched inside the trunk and started to breathe heavily, activating the senso-circuits.

Immediately the statue came to life. About twelve feet high, it was shaped like an enormous metal totem topped by two heraldic wings. The microphones in the wing-tips were powerful enough to pick up respiratory noises at a distance of twenty feet. There were four people well within focus, and the statue began to emit a series of low rhythmic pulses.

Seeing the statue respond to her, Lunora came forwards

with interest. Nevers backed away discreetly, taking Mme Charcot with him, leaving Lunora and I together, separated by a thin metal skin and three feet of vibrating air. Fumbling for some way of widening the responses, I eased up the control slides that lifted the volume. Neurophonics has never been my strong suit – I regard myself, in an old-fashioned way, as a sculptor, not an electrician – and the statue was only equipped to play back a simple sequence of chord variations on the sonic profile in focus.

Knowing that Lunora would soon realize that the statue's repertory was too limited for her, I picked up the hand-mike used for testing the circuits and on the spur of the moment began to croon the refrain from Creole Love Call. Reinterpreted by the sonic cores, and then relayed through the loudspeakers, the lulling rise and fall was pleasantly soothing, the electronic overtones disguising my voice and amplifying the tremors of emotion as I screwed up my courage (the statue was priced at five thousand dollars – even subtracting Nevers's 90 per cent commission left me with enough for the bus fare home).

Stepping up to the statue, Lunora listened to it motionlessly, eyes wide with astonishment, apparently assuming that it was reflecting, like a mirror, its subjective impressions of herself. Rapidly running out of breath, my speeding pulse lifting the tempo, I repeated the refrain over and over again, varying the bass lift to simulate a climax.

Suddenly I saw Nevers's black patent shoes through the hatch. Pretending to slip his hand into the control panel, he rapped sharply on the statue. I switched off.

'Don't please!' Lunora cried as the sounds fell away. She looked around uncertainly. Mme Charcot was stepping nearer with a curiously watchful expression.

Nevers hesitated. 'Of course, Miss Goalen, it still requires tuning, you –'

'I'll take it,' Lunora said. She pushed on her sunglasses, turned and hurried from the gallery, her face hidden.

Nevers watched her go. 'What happened, for heaven's sake? Is Miss Goalen all right?'

Mme Charcot took a cheque-book out of her blue crocodile handbag. A sardonic smirk played over her lips, and through the helix I had a brief but penetrating glimpse into her relationship with Lunora Goalen. It was then, I think, that I realized Lunora might be something more than a bored dilettante.

Mme Charcot glanced at her watch, a gold pea strung on her scrawny wrist. 'You will have it delivered today. By three o'clock sharp. Now, please, the price?'

Smoothly, Nevers said: 'Ten thousand dollars.'

Choking, I pulled myself out of the statue, and spluttered helplessly at Nevers.

Mme Charcot regarded me with astonishment, frowning at my filthy togs. Nevers trod savagely on my foot. 'Naturally, Mademoiselle, our prices are modest, but as you can see, M. Milton is an inexperienced artist.'

Mme Charcot nodded sagely. 'This is the sculptor? I am relieved. For a moment I feared that he lived in it.'

When she had gone Nevers closed the gallery for the day. He took off his jacket and pulled a bottle of absinthe from the desk. Sitting back in his silk waistcoat, he trembled slightly with nervous exhaustion.

'Tell me, Milton, how can you ever be sufficiently grateful to me?'

I patted him on the back. 'Georg, you were brilliant! She's another Catherine the Great, you handled her like a diplomat. When you go to Paris you'll be a great success. Ten thousand dollars!' I did a quick jig around the statue. 'That's the sort of redistribution of wealth I like to see. How about an advance on my cut?'

Nevers examined me moodily. He was already in the Rue de Rivoli, over-bidding for Leonardos with a languid flicker of a pomaded eyebrow. He glanced at the statue and shuddered. 'An extraordinary woman. Completely without taste. Which reminds me, I see you rescored the memory drum. The aria from *Tosca* cued in beautifully. I didn't realize the statue contained that.'

'It doesn't,' I told him, sitting on the desk. 'That was me. Not exactly Caruso, I admit, but then he wasn't much of a sculptor –'

'What?' Nevers leapt out of his chair. 'Do you mean you were using the hand microphone? You *fool!*'

'What does it matter? She won't know.' Nevers was groaning against the wall, drumming his forehead on his fist. 'Relax, you'll hear nothing.'

Promptly at 9.01 the next morning the telephone rang.

As I drove the pick-up out to Lagoon West Nevers's warnings rang in my ears – '... six international blacklists, sue me for misrepresentation ...' He apologized effusively to Mme Charcot, and assured her that the monotonous booming the statue emitted was most certainly not its natural response. Obviously a circuit had been damaged in transit, the sculptor himself was driving out to correct it.

Taking the beach road around the lagoon, I looked across at the Goalen mansion, an abstract summer palace that reminded me of a Frank Lloyd Wright design for an experimental department store. Terraces jutted out at all angles, and here and there were huge metal sculptures, Brancusi's and Calder mobiles, revolving in the crisp desert light. Occasionally one of the sonic statues hooted mournfully like a distant hoodoo.

Mme Charcot collected me in the vestibule, led me up a sweeping glass stairway. The walls were heavy with Dali and Picasso, but my statue had been given the place of honour at the far end of the south terrace. The size of a tennis court, without rails (or safety net), this jutted out over the lagoon against the skyline of Vermilion Sands, low furniture grouped in a square at its centre.

Dropping the tool-bag, I made a pretence of dismantling the control panel, and played with the amplifier so that the statue let out a series of staccato blips. These put it into the same category as the rest of Lunora Goalen's sculpture. A dozen pieces stood about on the terrace, most of them early period sonic dating back to the '70s, when sculptors produced an incredible sequence of grunting, clanking, barking and twanging statues, and galleries and public squares all over the world echoed night and day with minatory booms and thuds.

'Any luck?'

I turned to see Lunora Goalen. Unheard, she had crossed the terrace, now stood with hands on hips, watching me with interest. In her black slacks and shirt, blonde hair around her shoulders, she looked more relaxed, but sunglasses still masked her face.

'Just a loose valve. It won't take me a couple of minutes.' I gave her a reassuring smile and she stretched out on the chaise longue in front of the statue. Lurking by the french windows at the far end of the terrace was Mme Charcot, eyeing us with a beady smirk. Irritated, I switched on the statue to full volume and coughed loudly into the hand-mike.

The sound boomed across the open terrace like an artillery blank. The old crone backed away quickly.

Lunora smiled as the echoes rolled over the desert, the statues on the lower terraces responding with muted pulses. 'Years ago, when Father was away, I used to go on to the roof and shout at the top of my voice, set off the most wonderful echo trains. The whole place would boom for hours, drive the servants mad.' She laughed pleasantly to herself at the recollection, as if it had been a long time ago.

'Try it now,' I suggested. 'Or is Mme Charcot mad already?'

Lunora put a green-tipped finger to her lips. 'Carefully, you'll get me into trouble. Anyway, Mme Charcot is not my servant.'

'No? What is she then, your jailer?' We spoke mockingly, but I put a curve on the question; something about the Frenchwoman had made me suspect that she might have more than a small part in maintaining Lunora's illusions about herself.

I waited for Lunora to reply, but she ignored me and stared out across the lagoon. Within a few seconds her personality had changed levels, once again she was the remote autocratic princess.

Unobserved, I slipped my hand into the tool-bag and drew out a tape spool. Clipping it into the player deck, I switched on the table. The statue vibrated slightly, and a low melodious chant murmured out into the still air.

Standing behind the statue, I watched Lunora respond to the music. The sounds mounted, steadily swelling as Lunora moved into the statue's focus. Gradually its rhythms quickened, its mood urgent and plaintive, unmistakably a lover's passion-song. A musicologist would have quickly identified the sounds as a transcription of the balcony duet from *Romeo and Juliet*, but to Lunora its only source was the statue. I had recorded the tape that morning, realizing it was the only method of saving the statue. Nevers's confusion of *Tosca* and 'Creole Love Call' reminded me that I had the whole of classical opera in reserve. For ten thousand dollars I would gladly call once a day and feed in every aria from *Figaro* to *Moses and Aaron*.

Abruptly, the music fell away. Lunora had backed out of the statue's focus, and was standing twenty feet from me. Behind her, in the doorway, was Mme Charcot.

Lunora smiled briefly. 'It seems to be in perfect order,' she said. Without doubt she was gesturing me towards the door.

I hesitated, suddenly wondering whether to tell her the truth, my eyes searching her beautiful secret face. Then Mme Charcot came between us, smiling like a skull.

Did Lunora Goalen really believe that the sulpture was singing to her? For a fortnight, until the tape expired, it didn't matter. By then Nevers would have cashed the cheque and he and I would be on our way to Paris.

Within two or three days, though, I realized that I wanted to see Lunora again. Rationalizing, I told myself that the statue needed to be checked, that Lunora might discover the fraud. Twice during the next week I drove out to the summer-house on the pretext of tuning the sculpture, but Mme Charcot held me off. Once I telephoned, but again she intercepted me. When I saw Lunora she was driving at speed through Vermilion Sands in the Rolls-Royce, a dim glimmer of gold and jade in the back seat.

Finally I searched through my record albums, selected Toscanini conducting *Tristan and Isolde*, in the scene where Tristan mourns his parted lover, and carefully transcribed another tape.

That night I drove down to Lagoon West, parked my car by the beach on the south shore and walked out on to the surface of the lake. In the moonlight the summer-house half a mile away looked like an abstract movie set, a single light on the upper terrace illuminating the outlines of my statue. Stepping carefully across the fused silica, I made my way slowly towards it, fragments of the statue's song drifting by on the low breeze. Two hundred yards from the house I lay down on the warm sand, watching the lights of Vermilion Sands fade one by one like the melting jewels of a necklace.

Above, the statue sang into the blue night, its song never wavering. Lunora must have been sitting only a few feet above it, the music enveloping her like an overflowing fountain. Shortly after two o'clock it died down and I saw her at the rail, the white ermine wrap around her shoulders stirring in the wind as she stared at the brilliant moon.

Half an hour later I climbed the lake wall and walked along it to the spiral fire escape. The bougainvillaea wreathed through the railings muffled the sounds of my feet on the metal steps. I reached the upper terrace unnoticed. Far below, in her quarters on the north side, Mme Charcot was asleep.

Swinging on to the terrace, I moved among the dark statues, drawing low murmurs from them as I passed.

I crouched inside *Zero Orbit*, unlocked the control panel and inserted the fresh tape, slightly raising the volume.

As I left I could see on to the west terrace twenty feet below, where Lunora lay asleep under the stars on an enormous velvet bed, like a lunar princess on a purple catafalque. Her face shone in the starlight, her loose hair veiling her naked breasts. Behind her a statue stood guard, intoning softly to itself as it pulsed to the sounds of her breathing.

Three times I visited Lunora's house after midnight, taking with me another spool of tape, another love-song from my library. On the last visit I watched her sleeping until dawn rose across the desert. I fled down the stairway and across the sand, hiding among the cold pools of shadow whenever a car moved along the beach road.

All day I waited by the telephone in my villa, hoping she would call me. In the evening I walked out to the sand reefs, climbed one of the spires and watched Lunora on the terrace after dinner. She lay on a couch before the statue, and until long after midnight it played to her, endlessly singing. Its voice was now so strong that cars would slow down several hundred yards away, the drivers searching for the source of the melodies crossing the vivid evening air.

At last I recorded the final tape, for the first time in my own voice. Briefly I described the whole sequence of imposture, and quietly asked Lunora if she would sit for me and let me design a new sculpture to replace the fraud she had bought.

I clenched the tape tightly in my hand while I walked across the lake, looking up at the rectangular outline of the terrace.

As I reached the wall, a black suited figure put his head over the ledge and looked down at me. It was Lunora's chauffeur.

Startled, I moved away across the sand. In the moonlight the chauffeur's white face flickered bonily.

The next evening, as I knew it would, the telephone finally rang.

'Mr Milton, the statue has broken down again.' Mme Charcot's voice sounded sharp and strained. 'Miss Goalen is extremely upset. You must come and repair it. Immediately.'

I waited an hour before leaving, playing through the tape I had recorded the previous evening. This time I would be present when Lunora heard it.

Mme Charcot was standing by the glass doors. I parked in the court by the Rolls. As I walked over to her, I noticed how eerie the house sounded. All over it the statues were muttering to themselves, emitting snaps and clicks, like the disturbed occupants of a zoo settling down with difficulty after a storm. Even Mme Charcot looked worn and tense.

At the terrace she paused. 'One moment, Mr Milton. I will see if Miss Goalen is ready to receive you.' She walked quietly towards the chaise longue pulled against the statue at the end of the terrace. Lunora was stretched out awkwardly across it, her hair disarrayed. She sat up irritably as Mme Charcot approached.

'Is he here? Alice, whose car was that? Hasn't he come?'

'He is preparing his equipment,' Mme Charcot told her soothingly. 'Miss Lunora, let me dress your hair —'

'Alice, don't fuss! God, what's keeping him?' She sprang up and paced over to the statue, glowering silently out of the darkness. While Mme Charcot walked away Lunora sank on her knees before the statue, pressed her right cheek to its cold surface.

Uncontrollably she began to sob, deep spasms shaking her shoulders.

'Wait, Mr Milton!' Mme Charcot held tightly to my elbow. 'She will not want to see you for a few minutes.' She added: 'You are a better sculptor than you think, Mr Milton. You have given that statue a remarkable voice. It tells her all she needs to know.'

I broke away and ran through the darkness.

'Lunora!'

She looked around, the hair over her face matted with tears. She leaned limply against the dark trunk of the statue. I knelt down and held her hands, trying to lift her to her feet.

She wrenched away from me. 'Fix it! Hurry, what are you waiting for? Make the statue sing again!'

I was certain that she no longer recognized me. I stepped back, the spool of tape in my hand. 'What's the matter with her?' I whispered to Mme Charcot. 'The sounds don't really come from the statue, surely she realizes that?'

Mme Charcot's head lifted. 'What do you mean – not from the statue?'

I showed her the tape. 'This isn't a true sonic sculpture. The music is played off these magnetic tapes.'

A chuckle rasped briefly from Mme Charcot's throat. 'Well, put it in none the less, monsieur. She doesn't care where it comes from. She is interested in the statue, not you.'

I hesitated, watching Lunora, still hunched like a supplicant at the foot of the statue.

'You mean –?' I started to say incredulously. 'So you mean she's in love with the statue?'

Mme Charcot's eyes summed up all my naivety.

'Not with the statue,' she said. 'With *herself*.'

For a moment I stood there among the murmuring sculptures, dropped the spool on the floor and turned away.

They left Lagoon West the next day.

For a week I remained at my villa, then drove along the beach road towards the summer house one evening after Nevers told me that they had gone.

The house was closed, the statues standing motionless in the darkness. My footsteps echoed away among the balconies and terraces, and the house reared up into the sky like a tomb. All the sculptures had been switched off, and I realized how dead and monumental non-sonic sculpture must have seemed.

*Zero Orbit* had also gone. I assumed that Lunora had taken it with her, so immersed in her self-love that she preferred a clouded mirror which had once told her of her beauty to no mirror at all. As she sat on some penthouse veranda in Venice or Paris, with the great statue towering into the dark sky like an extinct symbol, she would hear again the lays it had sung.

Six months later Nevers commissioned another statue from me. I went out one dusk to the sand reefs where the sonic sculptures grow. As I approached, they were creaking in the wind whenever the thermal gradients cut through them. I walked up the long slopes, listening to them mewl and whine, searching for one that would serve as the sonic core for a new statue.

Somewhere ahead in the darkness, I heard a familiar phrase, a garbled fragment of a human voice. Startled, I ran on, feeling between the dark barbs and helixes.

Then, lying in a hollow below the ridge, I found the source. Half-buried under the sand like the skeleton of an extinct bird were twenty or thirty pieces of metal, the dismembered trunk and wings of my statue. Many of the pieces had taken root again and were emitting a thin haunted sound, disconnected fragments of the testament to Lunora Goalen I had dropped on her terrace.

As I walked down the slope, the white sand poured into my footprints like a succession of occluding hour glasses. The sounds of my voice whined faintly through the metal gardens like a forgotten lover whispering over a dead harp.

# Cry Hope, Cry Fury!

Again last night, as the dusk air moved across the desert from Vermilion Sands, I saw the faint shiver of rigging among the reefs, a topmast moving like a silver lantern through the rock spires. Watching from the veranda of my beach-house, I followed its course towards the open sand-sea, and saw the spectral sails of this spectral ship. Each evening I had seen the same yacht, this midnight schooner that slipped its secret moorings and rolled across the painted sea. Last night a second yacht set off in pursuit from its hiding place among the reefs, at its helm a pale-haired steerswoman with the eyes of a sad Medea. As the two yachts fled across the sand-sea I remembered when I had first met Hope Cunard, and her strange affair with the Dutchman, Charles Rademaeker...

Every summer during the season at Vermilion Sands, when the town was full of tourists and avant-garde film companies, I would close my office and take one of the beach-houses by the sand-sea five miles away at Ciraquito. Here the long evenings made brilliant sunsets of the sky and desert, crossing the sails of the sand-yachts with hieroglyphic shadows, signatures of all the strange ciphers of the desert sea. During the day I would take my yacht, a Bermuda-rigged sloop, and sail towards the dunes of the open desert. The strong thermals swept me along on a wake of gilded sand.

Hunting for rays, I sometimes found myself carried miles across the desert, beyond sight of the coastal reefs that presided like eroded deities over the hierarchies of sand and wind. I would drive on after a fleeing school of rays, firing the darts into the overheated air and losing myself in an abstract landscape composed of the flying rays, the undulating dunes and the triangles of the sails. Out of these materials, the barest geometry of time and space, came the bizarre figures of Hope Cunard and her retinue, like illusions born of that sea of dreams.

One morning I set out early to hunt down a school of white sand-rays I had seen far across the desert the previous day. For hours I moved over the firm sand, avoiding the sails of other yachtsmen, my only destination the horizon. By noon I was beyond sight of any landmarks, but I had found the white rays and sped after them through the rising dunes. The twenty rays flew on ahead, as if leading me to some unseen destination.

The dunes gave way to a series of walled plains crossed by quartz veins. Skirting a wide ravine whose ornamented mouth gaped like the door of a half-submerged cathedral, I felt the yacht slide to one side, a puncture in its starboard tyre. The air seemed to gild itself around me as I lowered the sail.

Kicking the flaccid tyre, I took stock of the landscape – submerged sand-reefs, an ocean of dunes, and the shell of an abandoned yacht half a mile away near the jagged mouth of a quartz vein that glittered at me like the jaws of a jewelled crocodile. I was twenty miles from the coast and my only supplies were a vacuum flask of iced Martini in the sail locker.

The rays, directed by some mysterious reflex, had also paused, settling on the crest of a nearby dune. Arming myself with the spear-gun, I set off towards the wreck, hoping to find a pump in its locker.

The sand was like powdered glass. Six hundred yards further on, when the raffia soles had been cut from my shoes, I turned back. Rather than exhaust myself, I decided to rest in the shade of the mainsail and walk back to Ciraquito when darkness came. Behind me, my feet left bloody prints in the sand.

I was sitting against the mast, bathing my torn feet in the cold Martini, when a large white ray appeared in the air overhead. Detaching itself from the others, who sat quietly on a distant crest, it had come back to inspect me. With wings fully eight feet wide, and a body as large as a man's, it flew monotonously around me as I sipped at the last of the lukewarm Martini. Despite its curiosity, the creature showed no signs of wanting to attack me.

Ten minutes later, when it still circled overhead, I took the spear-gun from the locker and shot it through its left eye. Transfixed by the steel bolt, its crashing form drove downwards into the sail, tearing it from the mast, and plunged through the rigging on to the deck. Its wing struck my head like a blow from the sky.

For hours I lay in the empty sand-sea, burned by the air, the giant ray my dead companion. Time seemed suspended at an unchanging noon, the sky full of mock suns, but it was probably in the early afternoon when I felt an immense shadow fall across the yacht. I lifted myself over the corpse beside me as a huge sand-schooner, its silver bowsprit as long as my own craft, moved through the sand on its white tyres. Their faces hidden by their dark glasses, the crew watched me from the helm.

Standing with one hand on the cabin rail, the brass portholes forming haloes at her feet, was a tall, narrow-hipped woman with blonde hair so pale she immediately reminded me of the Ancient Mariner's Nightmare Life-in-Death. Her eyes gazed at me like dark magnolias. Lifted by the wind, her opal hair, like antique silver, made a chasuble of the air.

Unsure whether this strange craft and its crew were an apparition, I raised the empty Martini flask to the woman. She looked down at me with eyes crossed by disappointment. Two members of the crew ran over to me. As they pulled the body of the sand-ray off my legs I stared at their faces. Although smooth-shaven and sunburnt, they resembled masks.

This was my rescue by Hope Cunard. Resting in the cabin

below, while one of the crew wrapped the wounds on my feet, I could see her pale-haired figure through the glass roof. Her preoccupied face gazed across the desert as if searching for some far more important quarry than myself.

She came into the cabin half an hour later. She sat down on the bunk at my feet, touching the white plaster with a curious hand.

'Robert Melville – are you a poet? You were talking about the Ancient Mariner when we found you.'

I gestured vaguely. 'It was a joke. On myself.' I could hardly tell this remote but beautiful young woman that I had first seen her as Coleridge's nightmare witch, and added: 'I killed a sand-ray that was circling my yacht.'

She played with the jade pendants lying in emerald pools in the folds of her white dress. Her eyes presided over her pensive face like troubled birds. Apparently taking my reference to the Mariner with complete seriousness, she said: 'You can rest at Lizard Key until you're better. My brother will mend your yacht for you. I'm sorry about the rays – they mistook you for someone else.'

As she sat there, staring through the porthole, the great schooner swept silently over the jewelled sand, the white rays moving a few feet above the ground in our wake. Later I realized that they had brought back the wrong prey for their mistress.

Within two hours we reached Lizard Key, where I was to stay for the next three weeks. Rising out of the thermal rollers, the island seemed to float upon the air, the villa with its terrace and jetty barely visible in the haze. Surrounded on three sides by the tall minarets of the sand-reefs, both villa and island had sprung from some mineral fantasy of the desert Rock spires rose beside the pathway to the villa like cypresses, pieces of wild sculpture growing around them.

'When my father first found the island it was full of gila

monsters and basilisks,' Hope explained as I was helped up the pathway. 'We come here every summer now to sail and paint.'

At the terrace we were greeted by the two other tenants of this private paradise – Hope Cunard's half-brother, Foyle, a young man with white hair brushed forwards over his forehead, a heavy mouth and pocked cheeks, who stared down at me from the balcony like some moody beach Hamlet; and Hope's secretary, Barbara Quimby, a plain-faced sphinx in a black bikini with bored eyes like two-way mirrors.

Together they watched me being brought up the steps behind Hope. The look of expectancy on their faces changed to polite indifference the moment I was introduced. Almost before Hope could finish describing my rescue they wandered off to the beach-chairs at the end of the terrace. During the next few days, as I lay on a divan nearby, I had more time to examine this strange menage. Despite their dependence upon Hope, who had inherited the island villa from her father, their attitude seemed to be that of palace conspirators, with their private humour and secret glances. Hope, however, was unaware of these snide asides. Like the atmosphere within the villa itself, her personality lacked all focus and her real attention was elsewhere.

Whom had Foyle and Barbara Quimby expected Hope to bring back? What navigator of the sand-sea was Hope Cunard searching for in her schooner with her flock of white rays? To begin with I saw little of her, though now and then she would stand on the roof of her studio and feed the rays that flew across to her from their eyries in the rock spires. Each morning she sailed off in the schooner, her opal-haired figure with its melancholy gaze scanning the desert sea. The afternoons she spent alone in her studio, working on her paintings. She made no effort to show me any of her work, but in the evenings, as the four of us had dinner together, she would stare at me over her liqueur as if seeing my profile within one of her paintings.

'Shall I do a portrait of you, Robert?' she asked one morning. 'I see you as the Ancient Mariner, with a white ray around your neck.'

I covered the plaster on my feet with the dragon-gold dressing-gown – left behind, I assumed, by one of her lovers. 'Hope, you're making a myth out of me. I'm sorry I killed one of your rays, but believe me, I did it without thinking.'

'So did the Mariner.' She moved around me, one hand on hip, the other touching my lips and chin as if feeling the contours of some antique statue. 'I'll do a portrait of you reading Maldoror.'

The previous evening I had treated them to an extended defence of the surrealists, showing off for Hope and ignoring Foyle's bored eyes as he lounged on his heavy elbows. Hope had listened closely, as if unsure of my real identity.

As I looked at the empty surface of the fresh canvas she ordered to be brought down from her studio, I wondered what image of me would emerge from its blank pigments. Like all paintings produced at Vermilion Sands at that time, it would not actually need the exercise of the painter's hand. Once the pigments had been selected, the photosensitive paint would produce an image of whatever still life or landscape it was exposed to. Although a lengthy process, requiring an exposure of at least four or five days, it had the immense advantage that there was no need for the subject's continuous presence. Given a few hours each day, the photosensitive pigments would anneal themselves into the contours of a likeness.

This discontinuity was responsible for the entire charm and magic of these paintings. Instead of a mere photographic replica, the movements of the sitter produced a series of multiple projections, perhaps with the analytic forms of cubism, or, less severely, a pleasant impressionistic blurring. However, these unpredictable variations on the face and form of the sitter were often disconcerting in their perception of character. The running of outlines, or separation of tonalities, could reveal tell-tale lines in the texture of skin and features, or generate strange swirls in the sitter's eyes like the epileptic spirals in the last demented landscapes of Van Gogh. These unfortunate effects were all too easily reinforced by any nervous or anticipatory movements of the sitter.

The likelihood that my own portrait would reveal more of my feelings for Hope than I cared to admit occurred to me as the canvas was set up in the library. I lay back stiffly on the sofa, waiting for the painting to be exposed, when Hope's half-brother appeared, a second canvas between his outstretched hands.

'My dear sister, you've always refused to sit for me.' When Hope started to protest Foyle brushed her aside. 'Melville, do you realize that she's never sat for a portrait in her life! Why, Hope? Don't tell me you're frightened of the canvas? Let's see you at last in your true guise.'

'Guise?' Hope looked up at him with wary eyes. 'What are you playing at, Foyle? That canvas isn't a witch's mirror.'

'Of course not, Hope.' Foyle smiled at her. 'All it can tell is the truth. Don't you agree, Barbara?'

Her eyes hidden behind her dark glasses, Miss Quimby nodded promptly. 'Absolutely. Miss Cunard, it will be fascinating to see what comes out. I'm sure you'll be very beautiful.'

'Beautiful?' Hope stared down at the canvas resting at Foyle's feet. For the first time she seemed to be making a conscious effort to take command of herself and the villa at Lizard Key. Then, accepting Foyle's challenge, and refusing to be outfaced by his broken-lipped sneer, she said: 'All right, Foyle. I'll sit for you. My first portrait – you may be surprised what it sees in me.'

Little did we realize what nightmare fish would swim to the surface of these mirrors.

During the next few days our portraits emerged like pale ghosts from the paintings. Each afternoon I would see Hope in the library, when she would sit for her portrait and listen to me reading from Maldoror, but already she was only interested in watching the deserted sand-sea. Once, when she was away, sailing the empty dunes with her white rays, I hobbled up to her studio. There I found a dozen of her paintings mounted on trestles in the windows, looking out on the desert below. Sentinels watching for Hope's phantom mariner, they revealed in monotonous detail the contours and texture of the empty landscape.

By comparison, the two portraits developing in the library were far more interesting. As always, they recapitulated in reverse, like some bizarre embryo, a complete phylogeny of modern art, a regression through the principal schools of the twentieth century. After the first liquid ripples and motion of a kinetic phase, they stabilized into the block colours of the hard-edge school, and from there, as a thousand arteries of colour irrigated the canvas, into a brilliant replica of Jackson Pollock. These coalesced into the crude forms of late Picasso, in which Hope appeared as a Junoesque madonna with massive shoulders and concrete face, and then through surrealist fantasies of anatomy into the multiple outlines of futurism and cubism. Ultimately an impressionist period emerged, lasting a few hours, a roseate sea of powdery light in which we seemed like a placid domestic couple in the suburban bowers of Monet and Renoir.

Watching this reverse evolution, I hoped for something in the style of Gainsborough or Reynolds, a standing portrait of Hope wearing floral scarlet under an azure sky, a pale-skinned English beauty in the grounds of her county house.

Instead, we plunged backwards into the netherworld of Balthus and Gustave Moreau.

As the bizarre outlines of my own figure emerged I was too surprised to notice the equally strange elements in Hope's portrait. At first glance the painting had produced a faithful if stylized likeness of myself seated on the sofa, but by some subtle emphasis of design the scene was totally transformed. The purple curtain draped behind the sofa resembled an immense velvet sail, collapsed against the deck of a becalmed ship, while the spiral bolster emerged as an ornamental prow. Most striking of all, the white lace cushions I lay against appeared as the plumage of an enormous sea-bird, hung around my shoulders like the anchor fallen from the sky. My own expression, of bitter pathos, completed the identification.

'The Ancient Mariner again,' Hope said, weighing my copy of Maldoror in her hand as she sauntered around the canvas. 'Fate seems to have type-cast you, Robert. Still, that's the role I've always seen you in.'

'Better than the Flying Dutchman, Hope?'

She turned sharply, a nervous tic in one corner of her mouth. 'Why did you say that?'

'Hope, who are you looking for? I may have come across him.'

She walked away from me to the window. At the far end of the terrace Foyle was playing some rough game with the sand-rays, knocking them from the air with his heavy hands and then pitching them out over the rock spires. The long stings whipped at his pock-marked face.

'Hope ...' I went over to her. 'Perhaps it's time I left. There's no point in my staying here. They've repaired the yacht.' I pointed to the sloop moored against the quay, fresh tires on its wheels. 'Besides ...'

'No! Robert, you're still reading Maldoror.' Hope gazed at me with her overlarge eyes, carrying out this microscopy of my face as if waiting for some absent element in my character to materialize.

For an hour I read to her, more as a gesture to calm her. For some reason she kept searching the painting which bore my veiled likeness as the Mariner, as if this image concealed some other sailor of the sand-sea.

When she had gone, hunting across the dunes in her schooner, I went over to her own portrait. It was then that I realized that yet another intruder had appeared in this house of illusions.

The portrait showed Hope in a conventional pose, seated like any heiress on a brocaded chair. The eye was drawn to her opal hair lying like a soft harp on her strong shoulders, and to her firm mouth with its slight reflective dip at the corners. What Hope and I had not noticed was the presence of a second figure in the painting. Standing against the skyline on the terrace behind Hope was the image of a man in a white jacket, his head lowered to reveal the bony plates of his forehead. The watery outline of his figure – the hands hanging at his sides were pale smudges – gave him the appearance of a man emerging from a drowned sea, strewn with blanched weeds and algae.

Astonished by this spectre materializing in the background of the painting, I waited until the next morning to see if it was some aberration of light and pigment. But the figure was there even more strongly, the bony features emerging through the impasto. The isolated eyes cast their dark gaze across the room. As I read to Hope after lunch I waited for her to comment on this strange intruder. Someone, plainly not her half-brother, was spending at least an hour each day before the canvas in order to imprint his image on its surface.

As Hope stood up to leave, the man's pensive face with its fixed eyes caught her attention. 'Robert – you have some kind of wild magic! You're there again!'

But I knew the man was not myself. The white jacket, the bony forehead and hard mouth were signatures of a separate subject. After Hope left to walk along the beach I went up to her studio and examined the canvases that kept watch for her on the landscape.

Sure enough, in the two paintings that faced the reefs to the south I found the mast of a waiting ship half-concealed among the sand-bars.

Each morning the figure emerged more clearly, its watching eyes seeming to come nearer. One evening, before going to bed, I locked the windows on to the terrace and draped a curtain over the painting. At midnight I heard something move along the terrace, and found the library windows swinging in the cold air, the curtain drawn back from Hope's portrait. In the painting the man's strong but melancholy face glared down at me with an almost spectral intensity. I ran on to the terrace. Through the powdery light a man's muffled figure moved with firm steps along the beach. The white rays revolved in the dim air over his head.

Five minutes later the white-haired figure of Foyle slouched from the darkness. His thick mouth moved in a grimace of morose humour as he shuffled past. On his black silk slippers there were no traces of sand.

Shortly before dawn I stood in the library, staring back at the watching eyes of this phantom visitor who came each night to keep his vigil by Hope's picture. Taking out my handkerchief, I wiped his face from the canvas, and for two hours stood with my own face close to the painting. Quickly the blurred paint took on my own features, the pigments moving to their places in a convection of tonalities. A travesty appeared before me, a man in a white yachtsman's jacket with strong shoulders and high forehead, the physique of some intelligent man of action, on which were superimposed my own plump features and brush moustache.

The paint annealed, the first light of the false dawn touching the sand-blown terrace.

'Charles!'

Hope Cunard stepped through the open window, her white gown shivering around her naked body like a tremulous wraith. She stood beside me, staring at my face on the portrait.

'So it *is* you. Robert, Charles Rademaeker came back as you ... The sand-sea brings us strange dreams.'

Five minutes later, as we moved arm in arm along the corridor to her bedroom, we entered an empty room. From a cabinet Hope took a white yachting-jacket. The linen was worn and sand-stained. Dried blood marked a bullet-hole in its waist.

I wore it like a target.

The image of Charles Rademaeker hovered in Hope's eyes as she sat on her bed like a tired dream-walker and watched me seal the windows of her bedroom.

During the days that followed, as we sailed the sand-sea together, she told me something of her affair with Charles Rademaeker, this Dutchman, recluse and intellectual who wandered across the desert in his yacht cataloguing the rare fauna of the dunes. Drifting out of the dusk air with a broken yard two years earlier, he had dropped anchor at Lizard Key. Coming ashore for cocktails, his stay had lasted for several weeks, a bizarre love-idyll between himself and this shy and beautiful painter that came to a violent end. What happened Hope never made clear. At times, as I wore the blood-stained jacket with its bullet-hole, I guessed that she had shot him, perhaps while she sat for a portrait. Evidently something strange had occurred to a canvas, as if it had revealed to Rademaeker some of the unstated elements he had begun to suspect in Hope's character. After their tragic climax, when Rademaeker had either been killed or escaped, Hope searched the sand-sea for him each summer in her white schooner.

Now Rademaeker had returned – whether from the desert or the dead – cast up from the fractured sand in my own person. Did Hope really believe that I was her reincarnated lover? Sometimes at night, as she lay beside me in the cabin, the reflected light of the quartz veins moving over her breasts like necklaces, she would talk to me as if completely aware of my separate identity. Then, after we had made love, she would deliberately keep me from sleeping, as if disturbed by even this attempt to leave her, and would call me Rademaeker, her clouded face that of a neurotic and disintegrating woman. At these moments I could understand why Foyle and Barbara Quimby had retreated into their private world.

As I look back now, I think I merely provided Hope with a respite from her obsession with Rademaeker, a chance to live out her illusion in this strange emotional pantomime. Meanwhile Rademaeker himself waited for us nearby in the secret places of the desert.

One evening I took Hope sailing across the dark sand-sea. I told the crew to switch on the rigging lights and the decorated bulbs around the deck awning. Driving this ship of light across the black sand, I stood with Hope by the stern rail, my arm around her waist. Asleep as she stood there, her head lay on my shoulder. Her opal hair lifted in the dark wake like the skeleton of some primeval bird.

An hour later, as we reached Lizard Key, I saw a white schooner slip its anchor somewhere among the sand-reefs and head away into the open sea.

Only Hope's half-brother was now left to remind me of my precarious hold on both Hope and the island. Foyle had kept out of my way, playing his private games among the rock spires below the terrace. Now and then, when he saw us walking arm in arm, he would look up from his beach chair with droll but wary eyes.

One morning, soon after I had suggested to Hope that she send her half-brother and Miss Quimby back to her house in Red Beach, Foyle sauntered into the library. I noticed the marked jauntiness of his manner. One hand pressed to his heavy mouth, he gestured sceptically at the portraits of Hope and myself. 'First the Ancient Mariner, now the Flying Dutchman – for a bad sailor you're playing an awful lot of sea roles, Melville. Thirty days in an open divan, eh? What are you playing next – Captain Ahab, Jonah?'

Barbara Quimby came up behind him, and the two of them smirked down at me, Foyle with his ugly faun's head.

'What about Prospero?' I rejoined evenly. 'This island is full of visions. With you as Caliban, Foyle.'

Nodding to himself at this, Foyle strolled up to the paintings. A large hand sketched in obscene outlines. Barbara Quimby began to laugh. Arms around each other's waists, they left together. Their tittering voices merged with the cries of the sand-rays wheeling above the rock spires in the blood-red air.

Shortly afterwards, the first curious changes began to occur to our portraits. That evening, as we sat together in the library, I noticed a slight but distinct alteration in the planes of Hope's face on the canvas, a pock-like disfigurement of the skin. The texture of her hair had altered, taking on a yellowish sheen.

This transformation was even more pronounced the following day. The eyes in the painting had developed a squint, as if the canvas had begun to recognize some imbalance within Hope's own gaze. I turned to the portrait of myself. Here, too, a remarkable change was taking place. My face had begun to develop a snout-like nose. The heavy flesh massed around the lips and nostrils, and the eyes were becoming smaller, submerged in the rolls of fat. Even my clothes had changed their texture, the black and white checks of my silk shirt resembling the suit of some bizarre harlequin.

By the next morning this ugly metamorphosis was so startling that even Hope would have noticed it. As I stood in the dawn light, the figures that looked down at me were those of some monstrous saturnalia. Hope's hair was now a bright yellow. The curled locks framed a face like a powdered skull. As for myself, my pig-snouted face resembled a nightmare visage from the black landscapes of Hieronymus Bosch.

I drew the curtain across the paintings, and then examined my mouth and eyes in the mirror. Was this mocking travesty how Hope and I really appeared? I decided that the pigments were faulty – Hope rarely renewed her stock – and were producing these diseased images of ourselves. After breakfast we dressed in our yachting clothes and went down to the quay. I said nothing to Hope. All day we sailed within sight of the island, not returning until the evening.

Shortly after midnight, as I lay beside Hope in her bedroom below the studio, I was woken by the white rays whooping through the darkness across the windows. They circled like agitated beacons. In the studio, careful not to wake Hope, I searched the canvases by the windows. In one I found the fresh image of a white ship, its sails concealed in a cove half a mile from the island.

So Rademaeker had returned, his presence in some way warping the pigments in our portraits. Convinced at the time by this insane logic, I drove my fists through the canvas, obliterating the image of the ship. My hands and arms smeared with wet paint, I went down to the bedroom. Hope slept on the crossed pillows, hands clasped over her breasts.

I took the automatic pistol which she kept in her bedside table. Through the window the white triangle of Rademaeker's sail rose into the night air as he raised his anchor.

Half way down the staircase I could see into the library. Arc lights had been set up on the floor. They bathed the canvases in their powerful light, accelerating the motion of the pigments. In front of the paintings, grimacing in obscene poses, were two creatures from a nightmare. The taller wore a black robe like a priest's cassock, a pig's papier-mâché mask on his head. Beside him was a woman in a yellow wig with a powdered face, bright lips and eyes. Together they primped and preened in front of the paintings.

Kicking back the door, I had a full glimpse of these nightmare figures. On the paintings the flesh ran like overheated wax, the images of Hope and myself taking up their own obscene pose. Beyond the blaze of arc lights the woman in the yellow wig slipped from the curtains on to the terrace. As I stepped over the cables I was aware briefly of a man's cloaked shoulders behind me. Something struck me below the ear. I fell to my knees, and the black robes swept over me to the window.

'Rademaeker!' Holding a paint-smeared hand to my neck, I stumbled over the pewter statuette that had struck me and ran out on to the terrace. The frantic rays whipped through the darkness like shreds of luminous spit. Below me, two figures ran down among the rock spires towards the beach.

Almost exhausted by the time I reached the beach, I walked clumsily across the dark sand, eyes stinging from the paint on my hands. Fifty yards from the beach the white sails of an immense sand-schooner rose into the night air, its bowsprit pointing towards me.

Lying on the sand at my feet were the remains of a yellow wig, a pig's plaster snout and the tattered cassock. Trying to pick them up, I fell to my knees. 'Rademaeker ...!'

A foot struck my shoulder. A slim, straight-backed man wearing a yachtsman's cap stared down at me with irritated eyes. Although he was smaller than I had imagined, I immediately recognized his sparse, melancholy face.

He pulled me to my feet with a strong hand. He gestured at the mask and costume, and at my paint-smeared arms.

'Now, what's this nonsense? What games are you people playing?'

'Rademaeker ...' I dropped the yellow-locked wig on to the sand. 'I thought it was –'

'Where's Hope?' His trim jaw lifted as he scanned the villa. 'Those rays ... Is she here? What is this – a black mass?'

'Damn nearly.' I glanced along the deserted beach, illuminated by the light reflected off the great sails of the schooner. I realized whom I had seen posturing in front of the canvas. 'Foyle and the girl! Rademaeker, they were there –'

Already he was ahead of me up the path, only pausing to shout to his two crewmen watching from the bows of the yacht. I ran after him, wiping the paint off my face with the wig. Rademaeker darted away from the path to take a short cut to the terrace. His compact figure moved swiftly among the rock spires, slipping between the sonic statues growing from the fused sand.

When I reached the terrace he was already standing in the darkness by the library windows, gazing in at the brilliant light. He removed his cap with a careful gesture, like a swain paying court to his sweetheart. His smooth hair, dented by the cap brim, gave him a surprisingly youthful appearance, unlike the hard-faced desert rover I had visualized. As he stood there watching Hope, whose white-robed figure was reflected in the open windows, I could see him in the same stance on his secret visits to the island, gazing for hours at her portrait.

'Hope . . . let me –'

Rademaeker threw down his cap and ran forward. A gunshot roared out, its impact breaking a pane in the french windows. The sound boomed among the rock spires, startling the rays into the air. Pushing back the velvet curtains, I stepped into the room.

Rademaeker's hands were on the brocaded sofa. He moved quietly, trying to reach Hope before she noticed him. Her back to us, she stood by the painting with the pistol in her hand.

Over-excited by the intense light from the arc lamps, the pigments had almost boiled off the surface of the canvas. The livid colours of Hope's pus-filled face ran like putrefying flesh. Beside her the pig-faced priest in my own image presided over her body like the procurator of hell.

Her eyes like ice, Hope turned to face Rademaeker and myself. She stared at the yellow wig in my hands, and at the paint smeared over my arms. Her face was empty. All expression had slipped from it as if in an avalanche.

The first shot had punctured the portrait of herself. Already the paint was beginning to run through the bullet-hole. Like a dissolving vampire, the yellow-haired lamia with Hope's features began to sway and spiral downwards.

'Hope ...' Rademaeker moved forward. Before he could take her wrist she turned and fired at him. The shot tore the glass from the window beside me. The fragments lay in the darkness like pieces of a broken moon.

The next shot struck Rademaeker in the left wrist. He dropped to one knee, gripping the bloodied wound. Confused by the explosions, which had almost jarred the pistol from her grip, Hope held the weapon in both hands, pointing it at the old bloodstain on my jacket. Before she could fire I kicked one of the arc lights across her feet. The room spun like a collapsing stage. I pulled Rademaeker by the shoulder on to the terrace.

We ran down to the beach. Half way along the path Rademaeker stopped, as if undecided whether to go back. Hope stood on the terrace, firing down at the rays that screamed through the darkness over our heads. The white schooner was already casting off, its sails lifting in the night air.

Rademaeker beckoned to me with his bloodied wrist. 'Get to the ship. She's alone now ... for ever.'

We crouched in the steering well of the schooner, listening to the sonic sculptures wail in the disturbed air as the last shots echoed across the empty desert.

At dawn Rademaeker dropped me half a mile from the beach at Ciraquito. He had spent the night at the helm, his bandaged wrist held like a badge to his chest, steering with his one strong hand. In the cold night air I tried to explain why Hope had shot at him, this last attempt to break through the illusions multiplying around her and reach some kind of reality.

'Rademaeker – I knew her. She wasn't shooting at you, but at a ... fiction of yourself, that image in the portrait. Damn it, she was obsessed with you.'

But he seemed no longer interested, his thin mouth with its uneasy lips making no reply. In some way he had disappoined me. Whoever finally took Hope away from Lizard Key would first have to accept the overlapping illusions that were the fabric of that strange island. By refusing to admit the reality of her fantasies Rademaeker had destroyed her.

When he left me among the dunes within sight of the beach-houses he gave a brusque salute and spun the helm, his erect figure soon lost among the rolling crests.

Three weeks later I chartered a yacht from one of the local ray-fishermen and went back to the island to collect my sloop. Hope's schooner was at its mooring. She herself, calm in her pale and angular beauty, came on to the terrace to greet me.

The paintings had gone, and with them any memory of that violent night. Hope's eyes looked at me with an untroubled gaze. Only her hands with their slim fingers moved with a restless life of their own.

At the end of the terrace her half-brother lounged among the beach chairs, Rademaeker's yachting cap propped over his eyes. Barbara Quimby sat beside him. I wondered whether to explain to Hope the callous and macabre game they had played with her, but after a few minutes she wandered away. Foyle's simpering mouth was the last residue of this world. Devoid of malice, he accepted his half-sister's reality as his own.

However, Hope Cunard has not entirely forgotten Charles Rademaeker. At midnight I sometimes see her sailing the sand-sea, in pursuit of a white ship with white sails. Last night, acting on some bizarre impulse, I dressed myself in the blood-stained jacket once worn by Rademaeker and sailed out to the edge of the sand-sea. I waited by a reef I knew she would pass. As she swept by soundlessly, her tall figure against the last light of the sun, I stood in the bows, letting her see the jacket. Again I wore it like a target.

Yet others sail this strange sea. Hope passed within fifty yards and never noticed me, but half an hour later a second yacht moved past, a rakish ketch with dragon's eyes on its bows and a tall, heavy-mouthed man wearing a yellow wig at its helm. Beside him a dark-eyed young woman smiled to the wind. As he passed, Foyle waved to me, and an ironic cheer carried itself across the dead sand to where I stood in my target-coat. Masquerading as mad priest or harpy, siren or dune-witch, they cross the sand-sea on their own terms. In the evenings, as they sail past, I can hear them laughing.

# Venus Smiles

Low notes on a high afternoon.

As we drove away after the unveiling my secretary said, 'Mr Hamilton, I suppose you realize what a fool you've made of yourself?'

'Don't sound so prim,' I told her. 'How was I to know Lorraine Drexel would produce something like that?'

'Five thousand dollars,' she said reflectively. 'It's nothing but a piece of old scrap iron. And the noise! Didn't you look at her sketches? What's the Fine Arts Committee for?'

My secretaries have always talked to me like this, and just then I could understand why. I stopped the car under the trees at the end of the square and looked back. The chairs had been cleared away and already a small crowd had gathered around the statue, staring up at it curiously. A couple of tourists were banging one of the struts, and the thin metal skeleton shuddered weakly. Despite this, a monotonous and high-pitched wailing sounded from the statue across the pleasant morning air, grating the teeth of passers-by.

'Raymond Mayo is having it dismantled this afternoon,' I said. 'If it hasn't already been done for us. I wonder where Miss Drexel is?'

'Don't worry, you won't see her in Vermilion Sands again. I bet she's half way to Red Beach by now.'

I patted Carol on the shoulder. 'Relax. You looked beautiful in your new skirt. The Medicis probably felt like this about Michelangelo. Who are we to judge?'

'*You* are,' she said. 'You were on the committee, weren't you?'

'Darling,' I explained patiently. 'Sonic sculpture is the thing. You're trying to fight a battle the public lost thirty years ago.'

We drove back to my office in a thin silence. Carol was annoyed because she had been forced to sit beside me on the platform when the audience began to heckle my speech at the unveiling, but even so the morning had been disastrous on every count. What might be perfectly acceptable at Expo 75 or the Venice Biennale was all too obviously passé at Vermilion Sands.

When we had decided to commission a sonic sculpture for the square in the centre of Vermilion Sands, Raymond Mayo and I had agreed that we should patronize a local artist. There were dozens of professional sculptors in Vermilion Sands, but only three had deigned to present themselves before the committee. The first two we saw were large, bearded men with enormous fists and impossible schemes – one for a hundred-foot-high vibrating aluminium pylon, and the other for a vast booming family group that involved over fifteen tons of basalt mounted on a megalithic step-pyramid. Each had taken an hour to be argued out of the committee room.

The third was a woman: Lorraine Drexel. This elegant and autocratic creature in a cartwheel hat, with her eyes like black orchids, was a sometime model and intimate of Giacometti and John Cage. Wearing a blue crêpe de Chine dress ornamented with lace serpents and other art nouveau emblems, she sat before us like some fugitive Salome from the world of Aubrey Beardsley. Her immense eyes regarded us with an almost hypnotic calm, as if she had discovered that very moment some unique quality in these two amiable dilettantes of the Fine Arts Committee.

She had lived in Vermilion Sands for only three months, arriving via Berlin, Calcutta and the Chicago New Arts Centre. Most of her sculpture to date had been scored for various Tantric and Hindu hymns, and I remembered her brief affair with a world-famous pop-singer, later killed in a car crash, who had been an enthusiastic devotee of the sitar. At the time, however, we had given no thought to the whining quarter-tones of this infernal instrument, so grating on the Western ear. She had shown us an album of her sculptures, interesting chromium constructions that compared favourably with the run of illustrations in the latest art magazines. Within half an hour we had drawn up a contract.

I saw the statue for the first time that afternoon thirty seconds before I started my speech to the specially selected assembly of Vermilion Sands notables. Why none of us had bothered to look at it beforehand I fail to understand. The title printed on the invitation cards – 'Sound and Quantum: Generative Synthesis 3' – had seemed a little odd, and the general shape of the shrouded statue even more suspicious. I was expecting a stylized human figure but the structure under the acoustic drapes had the proportions of a medium-sized radar aerial. However, Lorraine Drexel sat beside me on the stand, her bland eyes surveying the crowd below. A dream-like smile gave her the look of a tamed Mona Lisa.

What we saw after Raymond Mayo pulled the tape I tried not to think about. With its pedestal the statue was twelve feet high. Three spindly metal legs, ornamented with spikes and crosspieces, reached up from the plinth to a triangular apex. Clamped on to this was a jagged structure that at first sight seemed to be an old Buick radiator grille. It had been bent into a rough U five feet across, and the two arms jutted out horizontally, a single row of sonic cores, each about a foot long, poking up like the teeth of an enormous comb. Welded on apparently at random all over the statue were twenty or thirty filigree vanes.

That was all. The whole structure of scratched chromium had a blighted look like a derelict antenna. Startled a little by the first shrill whoops emitted by the statue, I began my speech and was about half way through when I noticed that Lorraine Drexel had left her seat beside me. People in the audience were beginning to stand up and cover their ears, shouting to Raymond to replace the acoustic drape. A hat sailed through the air over my head and landed neatly on one of the sonic cores. The statue was now giving out an intermittent high-pitched whine, a sitar-like caterwauling that seemed to pull apart the sutures of my skull. Responding to the boos and protests, it suddenly began to whoop erratically, the horn-like sounds confusing the traffic on the far side of the square.

As the audience began to leave their seats *en masse* I stuttered inaudibly to the end of my speech, the wailing of the statue interrupted by shouts and jeers. Then Carol tugged me sharply by the arm, her eyes flashing. Raymond Mayo pointed with a nervous hand.

The three of us were alone on the platform, the rows of overturned chairs reaching across the square. Standing twenty yards from the statue, which had now began to whimper plaintively, was Lorraine Drexel. I expected to see a look of fury and outrage on her face, but instead her unmoving eyes showed the calm and implacable contempt of a grieving widow insulted at her husband's funeral. As we waited awkwardly, watching the wind carry away the torn programme cards, she turned on a diamond heel and walked across the square.

No one else wanted anything to do with the statue, so I was finally presented with it. Lorraine Drexel left Vermilion Sands the day it was dismantled. Raymond spoke briefly to her on the telephone before she went. I presumed she would be rather unpleasant and didn't bother to listen in on the extension.

'Well?' I asked. 'Does she want it back?'

'No.' Raymond seemed slightly preoccupied. 'She said it belonged to us.'

'You and me?'

'Everybody.' Raymond helped himself to the decanter of Scotch on the veranda table. 'Then she started laughing.'

'Good. What at?'

'I don't know. She just said that we'd grow to like it.'

There was nowhere else to put the statue so I planted it out in the garden. Without the stone pedestal it was only six feet high. Shielded by the shrubbery, it had quietened down and now emitted a pleasant melodic harmony, its soft rondos warbling across the afternoon heat. The sitar-like twangs, which the statue had broadcast in the square like some pathetic love-call from Lorraine Drexel to her dead lover, had vanished completely, almost as if the statue had been rescored. I had been so stampeded by the disastrous unveiling that I had had little chance to see it and I thought it looked a lot better in the garden than it had done in Vermilion Sands, the chromium struts and abstract shapes standing out against the desert like something in a vodka advertisement. After a few days I could almost ignore it.

A week or so later we were out on the terrace after lunch, lounging back in the deck chairs. I was nearly asleep when Carol said, 'Mr Hamilton, I think it's moving.'

'What's moving?'

Carol was sitting up, head cocked to one side. 'The statue. It looks different.'

I focused my eyes on the statue twenty feet away. The radiator grille at the top had canted around slightly but the three stems still seemed more or less upright.

'The rain last night must have softened the ground,' I said. I listened to the quiet melodies carried on the warm eddies of air, and then lay back drowsily. I heard Carol light a cigarette with four matches and walk across the veranda.

When I woke in an hour's time she was sitting straight up in the deck chair, a frown creasing her forehead.

'Swallowed a bee?' I asked. 'You look worried.'

Then something caught my eye.

I watched the statue for a moment. 'You're right. It is moving.'

Carol nodded. The statue's shape had altered perceptibly. The grill had spread into an open gondola whose sonic cores seemed to feel at the sky, and the three stem-pieces were wider apart. All the angles seemed different.

'I thought you'd notice it eventually,' Carol said as we walked over to it. 'What's it made of?'

'Wrought iron – I think. There must be a lot of copper or lead in it. The heat is making it sag.'

'Then why is it sagging upwards instead of down?'

I touched one of the shoulder struts. It was springing elastically as the air moved across the vanes and went on vibrating against my palm. I gripped it in both hands and tried to keep it rigid. A low but discernible pulse pumped steadily against me.

I backed away from it, wiping the flaking chrome off my hands. The Mozartian harmonies had gone, and the statue was now producing a series of low Mahler-like chords. As Carol stood there in her bare feet I remembered that the height specification we had given to Lorraine Drexel had been exactly two metres. But the statue was a good three feet higher than Carol, the gondola at least six or seven across. The spars and struts looked thicker and stronger.

'Carol,' I said. 'Get me a file, would you? There are some in the garage.'

She came back with two files and a hacksaw.

'Are you going to cut it down?' she asked hopefully.

'Darling, this is an original Drexel.' I took one of the files. 'I just want to convince myself that I'm going insane.'

I started cutting a series of small notches all over the statue, making sure they were exactly the width of the file apart. The metal was soft and worked easily; on the surface there was a lot of rust but underneath it had a bright sappy glint.

'All right,' I said when I had finished. 'Let's go and have a drink.'

We sat on the veranda and waited. I fixed my eyes on the statue and could have sworn that it didn't move. But when we went back an hour later the gondola had swung right round again, hanging down over us like an immense metal mouth.

There was no need to check the notch intervals against the file. They were all at least double the original distance apart.

'Mr Hamilton,' Carol said. 'Look at this.'

She pointed to one of the spikes. Poking through the outer scale of chrome were a series of sharp little nipples. One or two were already beginning to hollow themselves. Unmistakably they were incipient sonic cores.

Carefully I examined the rest of the statue. All over it new shoots of metal were coming through: arches, barbs, sharp double helixes, twisting the original statue into a thicker and more elaborate construction. A medley of half-familiar sounds, fragments of a dozen overtures and symphonies, murmured all over it. The statue was well over twelve feet high. I felt one of the heavy struts and the pulse was stronger, beating steadily through the metal, as if it was thrusting itself on to the sound of its own music.

Carol was watching me with a pinched and worried look.

'Take it easy,' I said. 'It's only growing.'

We went back to the veranda and watched.

By six o'clock that evening it was the size of a small tree. A spirited simultaneous rendering of Brahms's *Academic Festival Overture* and Rachmaninoff's First Piano Concerto trumpeted across the garden.

'The strangest thing about it,' Raymond said the next morning, raising his voice above the din, 'is that it's still a Drexel.'

'Still a piece of sculpture, you mean?'

'More than that. Take any section of it and you'll find the original motifs being repeated. Each vane, each helix has all the authentic Drexel mannerisms, almost as if she herself were shaping it. Admittedly, this penchant for the late Romantic composers is a little out of keeping with all that sitar twanging, but that's rather a good thing, if you ask me. You can probably expect to hear some Beethoven any moment now – the Pastoral Symphony, I would guess.'

'Not to mention all five piano concertos – played at once,' I said sourly. Raymond's loquacious delight in this musical monster out in the garden annoyed me. I closed the veranda windows, wishing that he himself had installed the statue in the living room of his downtown apartment. 'I take it that it won't go on growing for ever?'

Carol handed Raymond another Scotch. 'What do you think we ought to do?'

Raymond shrugged. 'Why worry?' he said airily. 'When it starts tearing the house down cut it back. Thank God we had it dismantled. If this had happened in Vermilion Sands ...'

Carol touched my arm. 'Mr Hamilton, perhaps that's what Lorraine Drexel expected. She wanted it to start spreading all over the town, the music driving everyone crazy –'

'Careful,' I warned her. 'You're running away with yourself. As Raymond says, we can chop it up any time we want to and melt the whole thing down.'

'Why don't you, then?'

'I want to see how far it'll go,' I said. In fact my motives were more mixed. Clearly, before she left, Lorraine Drexel had set some perverse jinx at work within the statue, a bizarre revenge on us all for deriding her handiwork. As Raymond had said, the present babel of symphonic music had no connection with the melancholy cries the statue had first emitted. Had those forlorn chords been intended to be a requiem for her dead lover – or even, conceivably, the beckoning calls of a still unsurrendered heart? Whatever her motives, they had now vanished into this strange travesty lying across my garden.

I watched the statue reaching slowly across the lawn. It had collapsed under its own weight and lay on its side in a huge angular spiral, twenty feet long and about fifteen feet high, like the skeleton of a futuristic whale. Fragments of the *Nutcracker Suite* and Mendelssohn's 'Italian' Symphony sounded from it, overlaid by sudden blaring excerpts from the closing movements of Grieg's Piano Concerto. The selection of these hack classics seemed deliberately designed to get on my nerves.

I had been up with the statue most of the night. After Carol went to bed I drove my car on to the strip of lawn next to the house and turned on the headlamps. The statue stood out almost luminously in the darkness, booming away to itself, more and more of the sonic cores budding out in the yellow glare of the lights. Gradually it lost its original shape; the toothed grill enveloped itself and then put out new struts and barbs that spiralled upwards, each throwing off secondary and tertiary shoots in its turn. Shortly after midnight it began to lean and then suddenly toppled over.

By now its movement was corkscrew. The plinth had been carried into the air and hung somewhere in the middle of the tangle, revolving slowly, and the main foci of activity were at either end. The growth rate was accelerating. We watched a new shoot emerge. As one of the struts curved round a small knob poked through the flaking chrome. Within a minute it grew into a spur an inch long, thickened, began to curve and five minutes later had developed into a full-throated sonic core twelve inches long.

Raymond pointed to two of my neighbours standing on the roofs of their houses a hundred yards away, alerted by the music carried across to them. 'You'll soon have everyone in Vermilion Sands out here. If I were you, I'd throw an acoustic drape over it.'

'If I could find one the size of a tennis court. It's time we did something, anyway. See if you can trace Lorraine Drexel. I'm going to find out what makes this statue go.'

Using the hacksaw, I cut off a two-foot limb and handed it to Dr Blackett, an eccentric but amiable neighbour who sometimes dabbled in sculpture himself. We walked back to the comparative quiet of the veranda. The single sonic core emitted a few random notes, fragments from a quartet by Webern.

'What do you make of it?'

'Remarkable,' Blackett said. He bent the bar between his hands. 'Almost plastic.' He looked back at the statue. 'Definite circumnutation there. Probably phototropic as well. Hmm, almost like a plant.'

'Is it alive?'

Blackett laughed. 'My dear Hamilton, of course not. How can it be?'

'Well, where is it getting its new material? From the ground?'

'From the air. I don't know yet, but I imagine it's rapidly synthesizing an allotropic form of ferrous oxide. In other words, a purely physical rearrangement of the constituents of rust.' Blackett stroked his heavy brush moustache and stared at the statue with a dream-like eye. 'Musically, it's rather curious – an appalling conglomeration of almost every bad note ever composed. Somewhere the statue must have suffered some severe sonic trauma. It's behaving as if it had been left for a week in a railroad shunting yard. Any idea what happened?'

'Not really.' I avoided his glance as we walked back to the statue. It seemed to sense us coming and began to trumpet out the opening bars of Elgar's 'Pomp and Circumstance' march. Deliberately breaking step, I said to Blackett: 'So in fact all I have to do to silence the thing is chop it up into two-foot lengths?'

'If it worries you. However, it would be interesting to leave it, assuming you can stand the noise. There's absolutely no danger of it going on indefinitely.' He reached up and felt one of the spars. 'Still firm, but I'd say it was almost there. It will soon start getting pulpy like an over-ripe fruit and begin to shred off and disintegrate, playing itself out, one hopes, with Mozart's *Requiem* and the finale of the *Götterdämmerung*.' He smiled at me, showing his strange teeth. 'Die, if you prefer it.'

However, he had reckoned completely without Lorraine Drexel.

At six o'clock the next morning I was woken by the noise. The statue was now fifty feet long and crossing the flower beds on either side of the garden. It sounded as if a complete orchestra were performing some Mad Hatter's symphony out in the centre of the lawn. At the far end, by the rockery, the sonic cores were still working their way through the Romantic catalogue, a babel of Mendelssohn, Schubert and Grieg, but near the veranda the cores were beginning to emit the jarring and syncopated rhythms of Stravinsky and Stockhausen.

I woke Carol and we ate a nervous breakfast.

'Mr Hamilton!' she shouted. 'You've got to stop it!' The nearest tendrils were only five feet from the glass doors of the veranda. The largest limbs were over three inches in diameter and the pulse thudded through them like water under pressure in a fire hose.

When the first police cars cruised past down the road I went into the garage and found the hacksaw.

The metal was soft and the blade sank through it quickly. I left the pieces I cut off in a heap to one side, random notes sounding out into the air. Separated from the main body of the statue, the fragments were almost inactive, as Dr Blackett had stated. By two o'clock that afternoon I had cut back about half the statue and got it down to manageable proportions.

'That should hold it,' I said to Carol. I walked round and lopped off a few of the noisier spars. 'Tomorrow I'll finish it off altogether.'

I wasn't in the least surprised when Raymond called and said that there was no trace anywhere of Lorraine Drexel.

At two o'clock that night I woke as a window burst across the floor of my bedroom. A huge metal helix hovered like a claw through the fractured pane, its sonic core screaming down at me.

A half-moon was up, throwing a thin grey light over the garden. The statue had sprung back and was twice as large as it had been at its peak the previous morning. It lay all over the garden in a tangled mesh, like the skeleton of a crushed building. Already the advance tendrils had reached the bedroom windows, while others had climbed over the garage and were sprouting downwards through the roof, tearing away the galvanized metal sheets.

All over the statue thousands of sonic cores gleamed in the light thrown down from the window. At last in unison, they hymned out the finale of Bruckner's *Apocalyptic Symphony*.

I went into Carol's bedroom, fortunately on the other side of the house, and made her promise to stay in bed. Then I telephoned Raymond Mayo. He came around within an hour, an oxyacetylene torch and cylinders he had begged from a local contractor in the back seat of his car.

The statue was growing almost as fast as we could cut it back, but by the time the first light came up at a quarter to six we had beaten it.

Dr Blackett watched us slice through the last fragments of the statue. 'There's a section down in the rockery that might just be audible. I think it would be worth saving.'

I wiped the rust-stained sweat from my face and shook my head. 'No. I'm sorry, but believe me, once is enough.'

Blackett nodded in sympathy, and stared gloomily across the heaps of scrap iron which were all that remained of the statue.

Carol, looking a little stunned by everything, was pouring coffee and brandy. As we slumped back in two of the deck chairs, arms and faces black with rust and metal filings, I reflected wryly that no one could accuse the Fine Arts

Committee of not devoting itself wholeheartedly to its projects.

I went off on a final tour of the garden, collecting the section Blackett had mentioned, then guided in the local contractor who had arrived with his truck. It took him and his two men an hour to load the scrap – an estimated ton and a half – into the vehicle.

'What do I do with it?' he asked as he climbed into the cab. 'Take it to the museum?'

'No!' I almost screamed. 'Get rid of it. Bury it somewhere, or better still, have it melted down. As soon as possible.'

When they had gone Blackett and I walked around the garden together. It looked as if a shrapnel shell had exploded over it. Huge divots were strewn all over the place, and what grass had not been ripped up by the statue had been trampled away by us. Iron filings lay on the lawn like dust, a faint ripple of lost notes carried away on the steepening sunlight.

Blackett bent down and scooped up a handful of grains. 'Dragon's teeth. You'll look out of the window tomorrow and see the B Minor Mass coming up.' He let it run out between his fingers. 'However, I suppose that's the end of it.'

He couldn't have been more wrong.

Lorraine Drexel sued us. She must have come across the newspaper reports and realized her opportunity. I don't know where she had been hiding, but her lawyers materialized quickly enough, waving the original contract and pointing to the clause in which we guaranteed to protect the statue from any damage that might be done to it by vandals, livestock or other public nuisance. Her main accusation concerned the damage we had done to her reputation – if we had decided not to exhibit the statue we should have supervised its removal to some place of safekeeping, not openly dismembered it and then sold off the fragments to a scrap dealer. This deliberate affront had, her lawyers insisted, cost her commissions to a total of at least fifty thousand dollars.

At the preliminary hearings we soon realized that, absurdly, our one big difficulty was going to be proving to anyone who had not been there that the statue had actually started growing. With luck we managed to get several postponements, and Raymond and I tried to trace what we could of the statue. All we found were three small struts, now completely inert, rusting in the sand on the edge of one of the junkyards in Red Beach. Apparently taking me at my word, the contractor had shipped the rest of the statue to a steel mill to be melted down.

Our only case now rested on what amounted to a plea of self-defence. Raymond and myself testified that the statue had started to grow, and then Blackett delivered a long homily to the judge on what he believed to be the musical shortcomings of the statue. The judge, a crusty and short-tempered old man of the hanging school, immediately decided that we were trying to pull his leg. We were finished from the start.

The final judgment was not delivered until ten months after we had first unveiled the statue in the centre of Vermilion Sands, and the verdict, when it came, was no surprise.

Lorraine Drexel was awarded thirty thousand dollars.

'It looks as if we should have taken the pylon after all,' I said to Carol as we left the courtroom. 'Even the step-pyramid would have been less trouble.'

Raymond joined us and we went out on to the balcony at the end of the corridor for some air.

'Never mind,' Carol said bravely. 'At least it's all over with.'

I looked out over the rooftops of Vermilion Sands, thinking about the thirty thousand dollars and wondering whether we would have to pay it ourselves.

The court building was a new one and by an unpleasant irony ours had been the first case to be heard there. Much of the floor and plasterwork had still to be completed, and the balcony was untiled. I was standing on an exposed steel cross-beam; one or two floors down someone must have been driving a rivet into one of the girders, and the beam under my feet vibrated soothingly.

Then I noticed that there were no sounds of riveting going on anywhere, and that the movement under my feet was not so much a vibration as a low rhythmic pulse.

I bent down and pressed my hands against the beam. Raymond and Carol watched me curiously. 'Mr Hamilton, what is it?' Carol asked when I stood up.

'Raymond,' I said. 'How long ago did they first start on this building? The steel framework, anyway.'

'Four months, I think. Why?'

'Four.' I nodded slowly. 'Tell me, how long would you say it took any random piece of scrap iron to be reprocessed through a steel mill and get back into circulation?'

'Years, if it lay around in the wrong junkyards.'

'But if it had actually arrived at the steel mill?'

'A month or so. Less.'

I started to laugh, pointing to the girder. 'Feel that! Go on, feel it!'

Frowning at me, they knelt down and pressed their hands to the girder. They Raymond looked up at me sharply.

I stopped laughing. 'Did you feel it?'

'Feel it?' Raymond repeated. 'I can *hear* it. Lorraine Drexel – the statue. It's here!'

Carol was patting the girder and listening to it. 'I think it's humming,' she said, puzzled. 'It sounds like the statue.'

When I started to laugh again Raymond held my arm. 'Snap out of it, the whole building will be singing soon!'

'I know,' I said weakly. 'And it won't be just this building either.' I took Carol by the arm. 'Come on, let's see if it's started.'

We went up to the top floor. The plasterers were about to

move in and there were trestles and laths all over the place. The walls were still bare brick, girders at fifteen-foot intervals between them.

We didn't have to look very far.

Jutting out from one of the steel joists below the roof was a long metal helix, hollowing itself slowly into a delicate sonic core. Without moving, we counted a dozen others. A faint twanging sound came from them, like early arrivals at a rehearsal of some vast orchestra of sitar-players, seated on every plain and hilltop of the earth. I remembered when we had last heard the music, as Lorraine Drexel sat beside me at the unveiling in Vermilion Sands. The statue had made its call to her dead lover, and now the refrain was to be taken up again.

'An authentic Drexel,' I said. 'All the mannerisms. Nothing much to look at yet, but wait till it really gets going.'

Raymond wandered round, his mouth open. 'It'll tear the building apart. Just think of the noise.'

Carol was staring up at one of the shoots. 'Mr Hamilton, you said they'd melted it all down.'

'They did, angel. So it got back into circulation, touching off all the other metal it came into contact with. Lorraine Drexel's statue is here, in this building, in a dozen other buildings, in ships and planes and a million new automobiles. Even if it's only one screw or ball-bearing, that'll be enought to trigger the rest off.'

'They'll stop it,' Carol said.

'They might,' I admitted. 'But it'll probably get back again somehow. A few pieces always will.' I put my arm round her waist and began to dance to the strange abstracted music, for some reason as beautiful now as Lorraine Drexel's wistful eyes. 'Did you say it was all over? Carol, it's only just beginning. The whole world will be singing.'

# Say Goodbye to the Wind

At midnight I heard music playing from the abandoned nightclub among the dunes at Lagoon West. Each evening the frayed melody had woken me as I slept in my villa above the beach. As it started once again I stepped from the balcony on to the warm sand and walked along the shore. In the darkness the beachcombers stood by the tideline, listening to the music carried towards them on the thermal rollers. My torch lit up the broken bottles and hypodermic vials at their feet. Wearing their dead motley, they waited in the dim air like faded clowns.

The nightclub had been deserted since the previous summer, its white walls covered by the dunes. The clouded letters of a neon sign tilted over the open-air bar. The music came from a record-player on the stage, a foxtrot I had forgotten years before. Through the sand-strewn tables walked a young woman with coralline hair, crooning to herself as she gestured with jewelled hands to the rhythm of this antique theme. Her downward eyes and reflective step, like those of a pensive child, made me guess that she was sleepwalking, drawn to this abandoned nightclub from one of the mansions along the shore.

Beside me, near the derelict bar, stood one of the beachcombers. His dead clothes hung on his muscular body like the husk of some violated fruit. The oil on his dark chest lit up his drug-filled eyes, giving his broken face a moment of lucid calm. As the young woman danced by herself in her black nightgown he stepped forward and took her arms. Together they circled the wooden floor, her jewelled hand on his scarred shoulder. When the record ended she turned from him, her face devoid of expression, and walked among the tables into the darkness.

Who was my beautiful neighbour, moving with the certainty of a sleepwalker, who danced each evening with the beach-combers at the deserted nightclub? As I drove into Vermilion Sands the following morning I peered into the villas along the shore in the hope of seeing her again, but the beach was a zone of late-risers still asleep under their sealed awnings. The season at Vermilion Sands was now in full swing. Tourists filled the café terraces and the curio shops. After two or three hectic weeks at festivals devoted to everything from non-aural music to erotic food, most of them would jettison their purchases from their car windows as they sped back to the safety of Red Beach. Running to seed in the sand-reefs on the fringes of Vermilion Sands, the singing flowers and sculpture formed the unique flora of the landscape, an island ringed by strange sounds.

My own boutique, 'Topless in Gaza', which specialized in bio-fabric fashions, I had opened two years earlier. When I reached the arcade near Beach Drive at eleven o'clock that morning a small crowd was already peering through the window, fascinated by the Op Art patterns unfurling as the model gowns on display flexed and arched themselves in the morning sunlight. My partner, Georges Conte, his art nouveau eyepatch raised over his left eye, was settling an electric-yellow beach robe on to its stand. For some reason the fabric was unusually skittish, clinging to him like a neurotic dowager. Gripping the wrists with one hand, Georges forced it on to its stand, then stepped back before it could clutch at him again. The robe switched irritably from side to side, the fabric pulsing like an inflamed sun.

As I entered the shop I could see it was going to be one of our more difficult days. Usually I arrived to find the gowns and robes purring on their hangers like the drowsy inmates of an exquisite arboreal zoo. Today something had disturbed them. The racks of model dresses were seething, their patterns livid and discordant. Whenever they touched, the fabrics recoiled from each other like raw membranes. The beach-clothes were in an equal state of unrest, the bandanas and sun-suits throwing off eye-jarring patterns like exhibits in some demented kinetic art.

Hands raised in a gesture of heroic despair, Georges Conte came over to me. His white silk suit glimmered like a bilious rainbow. Even my own mauve day-shirt was unsettled, its seams beginning to shred and unravel.

'Georges, what's happening? The whole place is in uproar!'

'Mr Samson, I wash my hands of them! Sheer temperament, they're impossible to deal with!'

He looked down at his dappled sleeve, and tried to flick away the livid colours with a manicured hand. Upset by the disturbed atmosphere, his suit was expanding and contracting in irregular pulses, pulling across his chest like the fibres of a diseased heart. With a burst of exasperation he picked one of the model gowns from its rack and shook it angrily. 'Quiet!' he shouted, like an impresario calling an unruly chorus line to order. 'Is this "Topless in Gaza" or a demonic zoo?'

In the two years that I had known him Georges had always referred to the dresses and gowns as if they were a troupe of human performers. The more expensive and sensitive fabrics bred from the oldest pedigree stocks he would treat with the charm and savoir-faire he might have reserved for a temperamental duchess. At the opposite extreme, the flamboyant Op Art beachwear he handled with the cavalier charm he displayed to the teenage beauties who often strayed by accident into the boutique.

Sometimes I wondered if for Georges the gowns and suits were more alive than their purchasers. I suspected that he regarded the eventual wearers as little more than animated chequebooks whose sole function was to feed and exercise the exquisite creatures he placed upon their backs. Certainly a careless or offhand customer who made the mistake of trying to climb into a wrong fitting or, even worse, was endowed with a figure of less than Dietrich-like proportions, would receive brusque treatment from Georges and be directed with the shot of a lace cuff to the inert-wear shops in the town's amusement park.

This, of course, was a particularly bitter jibe. No one, with the exception of a few eccentrics or beachcombers, any longer wore inert clothing. The only widely worn inert garment was the shroud, and even here most fashionable people would not be seen dead in one. The macabre spectacle of the strange grave-flora springing from cracked tombs, like the nightmare collection of some Quant or Dior of the netherworld, had soon put an end to all forms of bio-fabric coffin-wear and firmly established the principle: 'Naked we came into this world, naked we leave it.'

Georges's devotion had been largely responsible for the success and select clientele of the boutique, and I was only too glad to indulge his whimsical belief in the individual personality of each gown and dress. His slim fingers could coax a hemline to shorten itself within seconds instead of hours, take in a pleat or enlarge a gusset almost before the customer could sign her cheque. A particularly exotic gown, unsettled by being worn for the first time or upset by the clammy contact of human skin, would be soothed and consoled by Georges as he patted it into place around its owner's body, his gentle hands caressing the nervous tissues around the unfamiliar contours of hip and bust.

Today, however, his charm and expertise had failed him. The racks of gowns itched and quivered, their colours running into blurred pools. One drawback of bio-fabrics is their extreme sensitivity. Bred originally from the gene stocks of delicate wisterias and mimosas, the woven yarns have brought with them something of the vine's remarkable response to atmosphere and touch. The sudden movement of someone nearby, let alone of the wearer, brings an immediate reply from the nerve-like tissues. A dress can change its colour and texture in a few seconds, becoming more décolleté at the approach of an eager admirer, more formal at a chance meeting with a bank manager.

This sensitivity to mood explains the real popularity of biofabrics. Clothes are no longer made from dead fibres of fixed colour and texture that can approximate only crudely to the vagrant human figure, but from living tissues that adapt themselves to the contours and personality of the wearer. Other advantages are the continued growth of the materials, fed by the body odours and perspiration of the wearer, the sweet liqueurs distilled from her own pores, and the constant renewal of the fibres, repairing any faults or ladders and eliminating the need for washing.

However, as I walked around the shop that morning I reflected that these immense advantages had been bought at a price. For some reason we had accumulated a particularly temperamental collection. Cases had been reported of sudden panics caused by the backfiring of an engine, in which an entire stock of model gowns had destroyed themselves in a paroxysm of violence.

I was about to suggest to Georges that we close the shop for the morning when I noticed that the first customer of the day had already arrived. Partly concealed by the racks of beachwear, I could only see an elegantly groomed face veiled by a wide-brimmed hat. Near the doorway a young chauffeur waited in the sunlight, surveying the tourists with a bored glance.

At first I was annoyed that a wealthy customer should arrive at the very moment when our stock was restive – I still remembered with a shudder the bikini of nervous weave that shed itself around its owner's ankles as she stood on the high diving-board above the crowded pool at the Neptune Hotel. I turned to ask Georges to use all his tact to get her to leave.

For once, however, he had lost his aplomb. Leaning forward from the waist, eyes focussed myopically, he was gazing at our customer like a seedy voyeur of the boulevards starstruck by some sub-teen nymphet.

'Georges! Pull yourself together! Do you know her?'

He glanced at me with blank eyes. 'What?' Already his suit had begun to smooth itself into a glass-like mirror, his invariable response when faced with a beautiful woman. He murmured: 'Miss Channing.'

'Who?'

'Raine Channing ...' he repeated. 'Before your time, Mr Samson, before anyone's time ...'

I let him walk past me, hands outstretched in the attitude of Parsifal approaching the Holy Grail. Certainly I remembered her, sometime international model and epitome of eternal youthfulness, with her melancholy, gamin face recreated by a dozen plastic surgeries. Raine Channing was a macabre relic of the 1970s and its teenage cult. Where, in the past, elderly screen actresses had resorted to plastic surgery to lift a sagging cheek or erase a tell-tale wrinkle, in the case of Raine Channing a young model in her early twenties had surrendered her face to the scalpel and needle in order to recapture the child-like bloom of a teenage ingénue. As many as a dozen times she had gone back to the operating theatre, emerging swathed in bandages that were rolled back before the arc lights to reveal a frozen teenage mask. In her grim way, perhaps she had helped to kill this lunatic cult. For some years now she had been out of the public eye, and I remembered only a few months beforehand reading about the death of her confidant and impresario, the brilliant couturier and designer of the first bio-fabric fashions, Gavin Kaiser.

Although now in her late twenties, Raine Channing still preserved her child-like appearance, this strange montage of adolescent faces. Her gaze reflected the suicides of Carole Landis and Marilyn Monroe. As she spoke to Georges in her low voice I realized where I had seen her, dancing with the beach-combers in the deserted nightclub at Lagoon West.

When I bought the boutique the faded fashion magazines had been filled with her photographs . . . Raine with her wounded eyes, looking out above the bandages around her remade cheeks, or wearing the latest bio-fabric creation at some exclusive discotheque, smiling into Kaiser's handsome gangster face. In many ways the relationship between Raine Channing and this twenty-five-year-old genius of the fashion houses summed up a whole disastrous epoch, of which Raine's mutilated face was a forgotten shrine. One day soon, before she reached the age of thirty, even that face would dissolve.

However, as she visited our boutique this grim prospect seemed a long way distant. Georges was delighted to see her, at last meeting on equal terms one of the too-bright luminaries of his apprenticeship. Without a thought for our disturbed stock, he opened the windows and display cases. Curiously, everything had quietened, the gowns stirring gently on their hangers like docile birds.

I waited for Georges to enjoy his moment of reminiscence, and then introduced myself.

'You've calmed everything down,' I congratulated her. 'They must like you.'

She drew her white fox collar around herself, rubbing her cheek against it. The fur slid around her neck and shoulders, nestling her in its caress. 'I hope so,' she said. 'Do you know, though, a few months ago I hated them? I really wanted everyone in the world to go naked, so that all the clothes would die.' She laughed at this. 'Now I've got to look for a whole new wardrobe.'

'We're delighted you've started here, Miss Channing. Are you staying long in Vermilion Sands?'

'A little while. I first came here a long time ago, Mr Samson.

Nothing in Vermilion Sands ever changes, have you noticed? It's a good place to come back to.'

We walked along the displays of gowns. Now and then she would reach out to stroke one of the fabrics, her white hand like a child's. As she opened her coat a sonic jewel, like a crystal rose, emitted its miniature music between her breasts. Velvet playtoys nestled like voles around her wrists. Altogether she seemed to be concealed in this living play-nest like a bizarre infant Venus.

What was it, though, about Raine Channing that so held me? As Georges helped her select a brilliant pastel gown, the other dresses murmuring on the chairs around her, it occurred to me that Raine Channing resembled a child-Eve in a couture-Eden, life springing from her touch. Then I remembered her dancing with the beachcombers in the deserted nightclub at Lagoon West.

While the young chauffeur carried out her purchases I said: 'I saw you last night. At the nightclub by the beach.'

For the first time she looked directly into my face, her eyes alert and adult above the white adolescent mask. 'I live nearby', she said, 'in one of the houses along the lake. There was music playing and people dancing.'

As the chauffeur opened the door of the car for her I saw that the seats were filled with playtoys and sonic jewels. They drove off together like two adults playing at being children.

Two days later I heard music coming again from the abandoned nightclub. As I sat on the veranda in the evening this faint night-music began, the dry metallic sounds muffled by the powdery air. I walked along the shore through the darkness. The beachcombers had gone, but Raine Channing wandered through the tables of the nightclub, her white gown drawing empty signatures in the sand.

A sand-yacht was beached in the shallows. Beside it a bare-chested young man watched with hands on hips. His powerful thighs stood out under his white shorts in the darkness, the thermal surf breaking the dust into ripples around his feet. With his broad face and smashed Michelangelesque nose he resembled some dark beach-angel. He waited as I approached, then stepped forward and walked past me, almost brushing my shoulder. The oil on his back reflected the distant lights of Vermilion Sands as he moved among the dunes towards the nightclub.

After this rendezvous I assumed that we would see no more of Raine Channing, but the next morning when I arrived at the shop in Vermilion Sands I found Georges waiting nervously by the door.

'Mr Samson, I tried to telephone you – Miss Channing's secretary has been calling, everything she bought has gone berserk! Nothing fits, three of the gowns are growing out of weave –'

I managed to calm him down, then spoke to Raine's secretary, a tart-toned Frenchwoman who sharply informed me that the entire wardrobe of two evening gowns, a cocktail dress and three day-suits which Raine had purchased from 'Topless in Gaza' had run to seed. Why this should have happened she had no idea. 'However, Mr Samson, I suggest you drive out immediately to Miss Channing's residence and either replace each item or reimburse the total purchase price of six thousand dollars. The alternative –'

'Mlle Fournier,' I insisted stiffly with what little pride I could muster, 'there is no alternative.'

Before I left, Georges brought out with elaborate care a cyclamen sports-suit in a shantung bio-fabric which he had ordered for one of our millionaire customers.

'For my good name, Mr Samson, if not for yours – at moments such as these one should show the flag.'

The suit clung to me like a willowy, lace-covered cobra, shaping itself to my chest and legs. Its colours glowed and rippled as it explored the contours of my body. As I walked out to my car people turned to look at this exquisite gliding snakeskin.

Five minutes after our arrival at Raine Channing's villa it had quietened down considerably, hanging from my shoulders like a wounded flower. The atmosphere at the villa seemed set for disaster. The young chauffeur who took my car whipped it away with a snarl of tyres, his eyes moving across my face like razors. Mlle Fournier greeted me with a peremptory nod. A sharp-faced Frenchwoman of about forty, she wore a witch-like black dress that seethed around her angular shoulders with the movements of a shrike.

'An entire wardrobe ruined, Mr Samson! Not only your own gowns, but priceless originals from Paris this season. We are out of our minds here!'

I did my best to calm her. One danger with bio-fabrics is that they are prone to stampede. Moments of domestic crisis, a cry of anger or even a door's slam, can set off a paroxysm of self-destruction. My own suit was already wilting under Mlle Fournier's baleful eye. As we went up the staircase I smoothed the ruffled velvet of the curtains, settling them into their niches. 'Perhaps they're not being worn enough,' I temporized. 'These fabrics do need human contact.'

Mlle Fournier gave me a surprisingly arch glance. We entered a suite on the top floor. Beyond the shaded windows was a terrace, the painted surface of the sand-lake below it. Mlle Fournier gestured at the open wardrobes in the large dressing-room. 'Human contact? Precisely, Mr Samson.'

Everywhere there was uproar. Gowns were strewn across the facing sofas. Several had lost all colour and lay blanched and inert. Others had felted, their edges curled and blackened like dead banana skins. Two evening dresses draped over the escritoire had run rogue, their threads interlocking in a macabre embrace. In the wardrobes the racks of gowns hung in restive files, colours pulsing like demented suns.

As we watched I sensed that they were uneasily settling themselves after some emotional outburst earlier that morning. 'Someone's been whipping them into a frenzy,' I told Mlle Fournier. 'Doesn't Miss Channing realize one can't play the temperamental fool near these fabrics?'

She gripped my arm, a barbed finger raised to my lips. 'Mr Samson! We all have our difficulties. Just do what you can. Your fee will be paid immediately.'

When she had gone I moved along the racks and laid out the more damaged dresses. The others I spaced out, soothing the disturbed fabrics until they relaxed and annealed themselves.

I was hunting through the wardrobes in the bedroom next door when I made a curious discovery. Packed behind the sliding doors was an immense array of costumes, faded models of the previous seasons which had been left to die on their hangers. A few were still barely alive. They hung inertly on their racks, responding with a feeble glimmer to the light.

What surprised me was their condition. All of them had been deformed into strange shapes, their colours bled like wounds across the fabric, reflecting the same traumatic past, some violent series of events they had witnessed between Raine Channing and whoever had lived with her in the years past. I remembered the clothes I had seen on a woman killed in a car crash at Vermilion Sands, blooming out of the wreckage like a monstrous flower of hell, and the demented wardrobe offered to me by the family of an heiress who had committed suicide. Memories such as these outlived their wearers. There was the apocryphal story of the murderer absconding in a stolen overcoat who had been strangled by the garment as it recapitulated the death-throes of its owner.

Leaving these uneasy relics to their dark end, I went back to the dressing-room. As I eased the last of the disturbed gowns on to their hangers the terrace door opened behind me.

Raine Channing stepped out of the sun. In place of her clinging white fur she now wore a bio-fabric bikini. The two yellow cups nestled her full breasts like sleeping hands. Despite the clear evidence of some fierce row that morning, she seemed composed and relaxed. As she stared at the now placid tenants of her wardrobe, her white face, like a devious adolescent's, more than ever resembled a surgical mask, the powdered child-face of a Manchu empress.

'Mr Samson! They're quiet now! You're like ...'

'St Francis calming the birds?' I suggested, still annoyed at having been summoned to Lagoon West. I gestured towards the sealed wardrobes in her bedroom. 'Forgive me saying so, but there are unhappy memories here.'

She picked up my jacket and draped it over her naked shoulders, a gesture of false modesty that none the less held a certain charm. The fabric clung to her like a pink flower, caressing her breasts and arms.

'The past is something of a disaster area, I'm afraid, Mr Samson. I know I brought you out here under false pretences. Something went wrong this morning, and you are the only neighbour I have.' She walked to the window and gazed over the painted lake. 'I came back to Vermilion Sands for reasons that must seem crazy.'

I watched her warily, but something about her apparent frankness destroyed caution. Presumably the midnight lover of the sand-yacht had left the scene, no doubt in a holocaust of emotions.

We went on to the terrace and sat in the reclining chairs beside the bar. During the next hours, and the many that followed in that house without mirrors above the painted lake, she told me something of her years with Gavin Kaiser, and how this young genius from the fashion world had found her singing at the open-air nightclub at Lagoon West. Seeing in this beautiful fifteen-year-old the apotheosis of the teenage cult, Kaiser had made her his star model for the bio-fabric fashions he designed. Four years later, at the age of nineteen, she had her first face lift, followed by even more extensive plastic surgery in the years immediately after. When Kaiser died she came back to Lagoon West, to the house near the deserted nightclub.

'I left so many pieces of myself behind in all those clinics and hospitals. I thought perhaps I could find them here.'

'How did Kaiser die?' I asked.

'From a heart attack – *they* said. It was some sort of terrible convulsion, as if he'd been bitten by a hundred rabid dogs. He was trying to tear his face to pieces.' She raised her hands to her own white mask.

'Wasn't there some doubt ...?' I hesitated.

She held my arm. 'Gavin was mad! He wanted nothing to change between us. Those face-lifts – he kept me at fifteen, but not because of the fashion-modelling. He wanted me for ever when I first loved him.'

At the time, however, I hardly cared why Raine Channing had come back to Lagoon West. Every afternoon I would drive out to her villa and we would lie together under the awning by the bar, watching the changing colours of the painted lake. There, in that house without mirrors, she would tell me her strange dreams, which all reflected her fears of growing young. In the evenings, as the music began to play from the deserted nightclub, we would walk across the dunes and dance among the sand-strewn tables.

Who brought this record-player to the nightclub with its one unlabelled disc? Once, as we walked back, I again saw the young man with the powerful shoulders and broken nose standing by his sand-yacht in the darkness. He watched us as we walked arm in arm, Raine's head against my chest. As she listened to the music jewel in her hand, Raine's eyes stared back like a child's at his handsome face.

Often I would see him at noon, sailing his sand-yacht across the lake a few hundred yards from the shore. I assumed that he was one of Raine's past lovers, watching his successor with a sympathetic curiosity and playing his music for us out of a bizarre sense of humour.

Yet when I pointed him out to Raine one afternoon she denied that she knew him or had even seen him before. Sitting up on one elbow, she watched the sand-yacht beached three hundred yards away along the shore. The young man was walking along the tideline, searching for something among the broken hypodermic vials.

'I can tell him to go away, Raine.' When she shook her head, I said: 'He was here. What happened between you?'

She turned on me sharply. 'Why do you say that?'

I let it pass. Her eyes followed him everywhere.

Two weeks later I saw him again at closer quarters. Shortly after midnight I woke on the terrace of Raine's villa and heard the familiar music coming from the deserted nightclub. Below, in the dim light, Raine Channing walked towards the dunes. Along the beach the thermal rollers whipped the white sand into fine waves.

The villa was silent. Mlle Fournier had gone to Red Beach for a few days, and the young chauffeur was asleep in his apartment over the garages. I opened the gates at the end of the dark, rhododendron-filled drive and walked towards the nightclub. The music whined around me over the dead sand.

The nightclub was empty, the record playing to itself on the deserted stage. I wandered through the tables, searching for any sign of Raine. For a few minutes I waited by the bar. Then, as I leaned over the counter, the slim-faced figure of the chauffeur stood up and lunged at me, his right fist aimed at my forehead.

Sidestepping into his arm, I caught his hand and rammed it on to the counter. In the darkness his small face was twisted in a rictus of anger. He wrenched his arm from me, looking away across the dunes to the lake. The music whined on, the record starting again.

I found them by the beach, Raine with her hand on the young man's hip as he bent down to cast off the yacht. Uncertain what to do, and confused by his off-hand manner as he moved around Raine, I stood among the dunes at the top of the beach.

Feet moved through the sand. I was staring down at Raine's face, its white masks multiplying themselves in the moonlight, when someone stepped behind me and struck me above the ear.

I woke on Raine's bed in the deserted villa, the white moonlight like a waiting shroud across the terrace. Around me the shadows of demented shapes seethed along the walls, the deformed inmates of some nightmare aviary. In the silence of the villa I listened to them tearing themselves to pieces like condemned creatures tormenting themselves on their gibbets.

I climbed from the bed and faced my reflection in the open window. I was wearing a suite of gold lamé which shone in the moonlight like the armour of some archangelic spectre. Holding my bruised scalp, I walked on to the terrace. The gold suit adhered itself to my body, its lapels caressing my chest.

In the drive Raine Channing's limousine waited among the rhododendrons. At the wheel the slim-faced chauffeur looked up at me with bored eyes.

'Raine!' In the rear seat of the car there was a movement of white-clad thigh, a man's bare-backed figure crouching among the cushions. Angered by having to watch the spectacle below in this preposterous suit, I started to tear it from my shoulders. Before I could shout again something seized my calves and thighs. I tried to step forward, but my body was clamped in a golden vice. I looked down at the sleeves. The fabric glowed with a fierce luminescence as it contracted around me, its fibres knotting themselves like a thousand zips.

Already breathing in uncertain spasms, I tried to turn, unable to raise my hands to the lapels that gripped my neck. As I toppled forwards on to the rail the headlamps of the car illuminated the drive.

I lay on my back in the gutter, arms clamped behind me. The golden suit glowed in the darkness, its burning light reflected in the thousand glass panes of the house. Somewhere below me the car turned through the gates and roared off into the night.

A few minutes later, as I came back to consciousness, I felt hands pulling at my chest. I was lifted against the balcony and sat there limply, my bruised ribs moving freely again. The bare-chested young man knelt in front of me, silver blade in hand, cutting away the last golden strips from my legs. The fading remnants of the suit burned like embers on the dark tiles.

He pushed back my forehead and peered into my face, then snapped the blade of his knife. 'You looked like a dying angel, Samson.'

'For God's sake ...' I leaned against the rail. A network of weals covered my naked body. 'The damn thing was crushing me ... Who are you?'

'Jason – Jason Kaiser. You've seen me. My brother died in that suit, Samson.'

His strong face watched me, the broken nose and broad mouth making a half-formed likeness.

'Kaiser? Do you mean your brother –' I pointed to the lamé rags on the floor. '– that he was strangled?'

'In a suit of lights. What he saw, God knows, but it killed him. Perhaps now you can make a guess, Samson. Justice in a way, the tailor killed by his own cloth.' He kicked the glowing shreds into the gutter and looked up at the deserted house. 'I was sure she'd come back here. I hoped she'd pick one of the beachcombers but you turned up instead. Sooner or later I knew she'd want to get rid of you.'

He pointed to the bedroom windows. 'The suit was in there somewhere, waiting to live through that attack again. You know, I sat beside her in the car down there while she was making up her mind to use it. Samson, she turns her lovers into angels.'

'Wait – didn't she recognize you?'

He shook his head. 'She'd never seen me – I couldn't stand my brother, Samson. Let's say, though, there are certain ciphers in the face, resemblances one can make use of. That record was all I needed, the old theme tune of the nightclub. I found it in the bar.'

Despite my bruised ribs and torn skin I was still thinking of Raine, and that strange child's face she wore like a mask. She had come back to Lagoon West to make a beginning, and instead found that events repeated themselves, trapping her into this grim recapitulation of Kaiser's death.

Jason walked towards the bedroom as I stood there naked. 'Where are you going?' I called out. 'Everything is dead in there.'

'I know. We had quite a job fitting you into that suit, Samson. They knew what was coming.' He pointed to the headlamps speeding along the lake road five miles to the south. 'Say goodbye to Miss Channing.'

I watched the car disappear among the hills. By the abandoned nightclub the dark air drew its empty signatures across the dunes. 'Say goodbye to the wind.'

# Studio 5, The Stars

Every evening during the summer at Vermilion Sands the insane poems of my beautiful neighbour drifted across the desert to me from Studio 5, The Stars, the broken skeins of coloured tape unravelling in the sand like the threads of a dismembered web. All night they would flutter around the buttresses below the terrace, entwining themselves through the balcony railings, and by morning, before I swept them away, they would hang across the south face of the villa like a vivid cerise bougainvillaea.

Once, after I had been to Red Beach for three days, I returned to find the entire terrace filled by an enormous cloud of coloured tissues, which burst through the french windows as I opened them and pushed into the lounge, spreading across the furniture and bookcases like the delicate tendrils of some vast and gentle plant. For days afterwards I found fragments of the poems everywhere.

I complained several times, walking the three hundred yards across the dunes to deliver a letter of protest, but no one ever answered the bell. I had only once seen my neighbour, on the day she arrived, driving down the Stars in a huge El Dorado convertible, her long hair swept behind her like the head-dress of a goddess. She had vanished in a glimmer of speed, leaving me with a fleeting image of sudden eyes in an ice-white face.

Why she refused to answer her bell I could never understand, but I noticed that each time I walked across to Studio 5 the sky was full of sand-rays, wheeling and screeching like anguished bats. On the last occasion, as I stood by her black glass front door, deliberately pressing the bell into its socket, a giant sand-ray had fallen out of the sky at my feet.

But this, as I realized later, was the crazy season at Vermilion Sands, when Tony Sapphire heard a sand-ray singing, and I saw the god Pan drive by in a Cadillac.

Who was Aurora Day, I often ask myself now. Sweeping across the placid out-of-season sky like a summer comet, she seems to have appeared in a different role to each of us at the colony along the Stars. To me, at first, she was a beautiful neurotic disguised as a *femme fatale*, but Raymond Mayo saw her as one of Salvador Dali's exploding madonnas, an enigma serenely riding out the apocalypse. To Tony Sapphire and the rest of her followers along the beach she was a reincarnation of Astarte herself, a diamond-eyed time-child thirty centuries old.

I can remember clearly how I found the first of her poems. After dinner one evening I was resting on the terrace – something I did most of the time at Vermilion Sands – when I noticed a streamer lying on the sand below the railing. A few yards away were several others, and for half an hour I watched them being blown lightly across the dunes. A car's headlamps shone in the drive at Studio 5, and I assumed that a new tenant had moved into the villa, which had stood empty for several months.

Finally, out of curiosity, I straddled the rail, jumped down on to the sand and picked up one of the ribbons of pink tissue. It was a fragment about three feet long, the texture of rose petal, so light that it began to flake and dissolve in my fingers. Holding it up I read: ... COMPARE THEE TO A SUMMER'S DAY, THOU ART MORE LOVELY ...

I let it flutter away into the darkness below the balcony, then bent down and carefully picked up another, disentangling it from one of the buttresses.

Printed along it in the same ornate neo-classical type was: ... SET KEEL TO BREAKERS, FORTH ON THAT GODLY SEA ...

I looked over my shoulder. The light over the desert had

gone now, and three hundred yards away my neighbour's villa was lit like a spectral crown. The exposed quartz veins in the sand reefs along the Stars rippled like necklaces in the sweeping headlights of the cars driving into Red Beach.

I glanced at the tape again.

Shakespeare and Ezra Pound? My neighbour had the most curious tastes. My interest fading, I returned to the terrace.

Over the next few days the streamers continued to blow across the dunes, for some reason always starting in the evening, when the lights of the traffic illuminated the lengths of coloured gauze. But to begin with I hardly noticed them – I was then editing *Wave IX*, an avant-garde poetry review, and the studio was full of auto-tapes and old galley proofs. Nor was I particularly surprised to find I had a poetess for my neighbour. Almost all the studios along the Stars are occupied by painters and poets – the majority abstract and non-productive. Most of us were suffering from various degrees of beach fatigue, that chronic malaise which exiles the victim to a limbo of endless sunbathing, dark glasses and afternoon terraces.

Later, however, the streamers drifting across the sand became rather more of a nuisance. When the protest notes achieved nothing I went over to my neighbour's villa with a view to seeing her in person. On this last occasion, after a dying ray had plummeted out of the sky and nearly stung me in its final spasm, I realized that there was little chance of reaching her.

A hunchbacked chauffeur with a club foot and a twisted face like a senile faun's was cleaning the cerise Cadillac in the drive. I went over to him and pointed to the strands of tissue trailing through the first-floor windows and falling on to the desert below.

'These tapes are blowing all over my villa,' I told him. 'Your mistress must have one of her VT sets on open sequence.'

He eyed me across the broad hood of the El Dorado, sat down in the driving seat and took a small flute from the dashboard.

As I walked round to him he began to play some high, irritating chords. I waited until he had finished and asked in a louder voice: 'Do you mind telling her to close the windows?'

He ignored me, his lips pressed moodily to the flute. I bent down and was about to shout into his ear when a gust of wind swirled across one of the dunes just beyond the drive, in an instant whirled over the gravel, flinging up a miniature tornado of dust and ash. This miniature tornado completely enclosed us, blinding my eyes and filling my mouth with grit. Arms shielding my face, I moved away towards the drive, the long streamers whipping around me.

As suddenly as it had started, the squall vanished. The dust stilled and faded, leaving the air as motionless as it had been a few moments previously. I saw that I had backed about thirty yards down the drive, and to my astonishment realized that the Cadillac and chauffeur had disappeared, although the garage door was still open.

My head rang strangely, and I felt irritable and short of breath. I was about to approach the house again, annoyed at having been refused entry and left to suffer the full filthy impact of the dust squall, when I heard the thin piping refrain sound again into the air.

Low, but clear and strangely menacing, it sang in my ears, the planes of sound shifting about me in the air. Looking around for its source, I noticed the dust flicking across the surface of the dunes on either side of the drive.

Without waiting, I turned on my heel and hurried back to my villa.

Angry with myself for having been made such a fool of, and resolved to press some formal complaint, I first went around the terrace, picking up all the strands of tissue and stuffing them into the disposal chute. I climbed below the villa and cut away the tangled masses of streamers.

Cursorily, I read a few of the tapes at random. All printed the same erratic fragments, intact phrases from Shakespeare, Wordsworth, Keats and Eliot. My neighbour's VT set appeared to have a drastic memory fault, and instead of producing a variant on the classical model the selector head was simply regurgitating a dismembered version of the model itself. For a moment I thought seriously of telephoning the IBM agency in Red Beach and asking them to send a repair man round.

That evening, however, I finally spoke to my neighbour in person.

I had gone to sleep at about eleven, and an hour or so later something woke me. A bright moon was at apogee, moving behind strands of pale green cloud that cast a thin light over the desert and the Stars. I stepped out on to the veranda and immediately noticed a curiously luminescent glow moving between the dunes. Like the strange music I had heard from the chauffeur's flute, the glow appeared to be sourceless, but I assumed it was cast by the moon shining through a narrow interval between the clouds.

Then I saw her, appearing for a moment among the dunes, strolling across the midnight sand. She wore a long white gown that billowed out behind her, against which her blue hair drifted loosely in the wind like the tail-fan of a paradise bird. Streamers floated about her feet, and overhead two or three purple rays circled endlessly. She walked on, apparently unaware of them, a single light behind her shining through an upstairs window of her villa.

Belting my dressing-gown, I leaned against a pillar and watched her quietly, for the moment forgiving her the streamers and her ill-trained chauffeur. Occasionally she disappeared behind one of the green-shadowed dunes, her head raised slightly, moving from the boulevard towards the sand reefs on the edge of the fossil lake.

She was about a hundred yards from the nearest sand reef, a long inverted gallery of winding groins and over-hanging grottoes, when something about her straight path and regular unvarying pace made me wonder whether she might in fact be sleepwalking.

I hesitated briefly, watching the rays circling around her head, then jumped over the rail and ran across the sand towards her.

The quartz flints stung at my bare feet, but I managed to reach her just as she neared the edge of the reef. I broke into a walk beside her and touched her elbow.

Three feet above my head the rays spat and whirled in the darkness. The strange luminosity that I had assumed came from the moon seemed rather to emanate from her white gown.

My neighbour was not somnambulating, as I thought, but lost in some deep reverie or dream. Her black eyes stared opaquely in front of her, her slim white-skinned face like a marble mask, motionless and without expression. She looked round at me sightlessly, one hand gesturing me away. Suddenly she stopped and glanced down at her feet, abruptly becoming aware of herself and her midnight walk. Her eyes cleared and she saw the mouth of the sand reef. She stepped back involuntarily, the light radiating from her gown increasing with her alarm.

Overhead the rays soared upwards into the air, their arcs wider now that she was awake.

'Sorry to startle you,' I apologized. 'But you were getting too close to the reef.'

She pulled away from me, her long black eyebrows arching.

'What?' she said uncertainly. 'Who are you?' To herself, as if completing her dream, she murmured *sotto voce*: 'Oh God,

Paris, choose me, not Minerva –' She broke off and stared at me wildly, her carmine lips fretting. She strode off across the sand, the rays swinging like pendulums through the dim air above her, taking with her the pool of amber light.

I waited until she reached her villa and turned away. Glancing at the ground, I noticed something glitter in the small depression formed by one of her footprints. I bent down, picked up a small jewel, a perfectly cut diamond of a single carat, then saw another in the next footprint. Hurrying forwards, I picked up half-a-dozen of the jewels, and was about to call out after her disappearing figure when I felt something wet in my hand.

Where I had held the jewels in the hollow of my palm now swam a pool of ice-cold dew.

I found out who she was the next day.

After breakfast I was in the bar when I saw the El Dorado turn into the drive. The club-footed chauffeur jumped from the car and hobbled over in his curious swinging gait to the front door. In his black-gloved hand he carried a pink envelope. I let him wait a few minutes, then opened the letter on the step as he went back to the car and sat waiting for me, his engine running.

> I'm sorry to have been so rude last night. You stepped right into my dream and startled me. Could I make amends by offering you a cocktail? My chauffeur will collect you at noon.
>
> AURORA DAY

I looked at my watch. It was 11:55. The five minutes, presumably, gave me time to compose myself.

The chauffeur was studying his driving wheel, apparently indifferent to my reaction. Leaving the door open, I stepped inside and put on my beach-jacket. On the way out I slipped a proof copy of *Wave IX* into one of the pockets.

The chauffeur barely waited for me to climb in before moving the big car rapidly down the drive.

'How long are you staying in Vermilion Sands?' I asked, addressing the band of curly russet hair between the peaked cap and black collar.

He said nothing. As we drove along the Stars he suddenly cut out into the oncoming lane and gunned the Cadillac forward in a tremendous burst of speed to overtake a car ahead.

Settling myself, I put the question again and waited for him to reply, then smartly tapped his black serge shoulder.

'Are you deaf, or just rude?'

For a second he took his eyes off the road and glanced back at me. I had a momentary impression of bright red pupils, ribald eyes that regarded me with a mixture of contempt and unconcealed savagery. Out of the side of his mouth came a sudden cackling stream of violent imprecations, a short filthy blast that sent me back into my seat.

He jumped out when we reached Studio 5 and opened the door for me, beckoning me up the black marble steps like an attendant spider ushering a very small fly into a particularly large web.

Once inside the doorway he seemed to disappear. I walked through the softly lit hall towards an interior pool where a fountain played and white carp circled tirelessly. Beyond it, in the lounge, I could see my neighbour reclining on a chaise longue, her white gown spread around her like a fan, the jewels embroidered into it glittering in the fountain light.

As I sat down she regarded me curiously, putting away a slender volume bound in yellow calf which appeared to be a private edition of poems. Scattered across the floor beside her was a miscellaneous array of other volumes, many of which I could identify as recently printed collections and anthologies.

I noticed a few coloured streamers trailing through the curtains by the window, and glanced around to see where she kept her VT set, helping myself to a cocktail off the low table between us.

'Do you read a lot of poetry?' I asked, indicating the volumes around her.

She nodded. 'As much as I can bear to.'

I laughed. 'I know what you mean. I have to read rather more than I want.' I took a copy of *Wave IX* from my pocket and passed it to her. 'Have you come across this one?'

She glanced at the title page, her manner moody and autocratic. I wondered why she had bothered to ask me over. 'Yes, I have. Appalling, isn't it? "Paul Ransom" ', she noted. 'Is that you? You're the editor? How interesting.'

She said it with a peculiar inflection, apparently considering some possible course of action. For a moment she watched me reflectively. Her personality seemed totally dissociated, her awareness of me varying abruptly from one level to another, like light-changes in a bad motion picture. However, although her mask-like face remained motionless, I none the less detected a quickening of interest.

'Well, tell me about your work. You must know so much about what is wrong with modern poetry. Why is it all so bad?'

I shrugged. 'I suppose its principally a matter of inspiration. I used to write a fair amount myself years ago, but the impulse faded as soon as I could afford a VT set. In the old days a poet had to sacrifice himself in order to master his medium. Now that technical mastery is simply a question of pushing a button, selecting metre, rhyme, assonance on a dial, there's no need for sacrifice, no ideal to invent to make the sacrifice worthwhile –'

I broke off. She was watching me in a remarkably alert way, almost as if she were going to swallow me.

Changing the tempo, I said: 'I've read quite a lot of your

poetry, too. Forgive me mentioning it, but I think there's something wrong with your Verse-Transcriber.'

Her face snapped and she looked away from me irritably. 'I haven't got one of those dreadful machines. Heavens above, you don't think *I* would use one?'

'Then where do the tapes come from?' I asked. 'The streamers that drift across every evening. They're covered with fragments of verse.'

Off-handedly, she said: 'Are they? Oh, I didn't know.' She looked down at the volumes scattered about on the floor. 'Although I should be the last person to write verse, I have been forced to recently. Through sheer necessity, you see, to preserve a dying art.'

She had baffled me completely. As far as I could remember, most of the poems on the tapes had already been written.

She glanced up and gave me a vivid smile.

'I'll send you some.'

The first ones arrived the next morning. They were delivered by the chauffeur in the pink Cadillac, neatly printed on quarto vellum and sealed by a floral ribbon. Most of the poems submitted to me come through the post on computer punch-tape, rolled up like automat tickets, and it was certainly a pleasure to receive such elegant manuscripts.

The poems, however, were impossibly bad. There were six in all, two Petrarchan sonnets, an ode and three free-form longer pieces. All were written in the same hectoring tone, at once minatory and obscure, like the oracular deliriums of an insane witch. Their overall import was strangely disturbing, not so much for the content of the poems as for the deranged mind behind them. Aurora Day was obviously living in a private world which she took very seriously indeed. I decided that she was a wealthy neurotic able to over-indulge her private fantasies.

I flipped through the sheets, smelling the musk-like scent that misted up from them. Where had she unearthed this curious style, these archaic mannerisms, the 'arise, earthly seers, and to thy ancient courses pen now thy truest vows'? Mixed up in some of the metaphors were odd echoes of Milton and Virgil. In fact, the whole tone reminded me of the archpriestess in the Aeneid who lets off blistering tirades whenever Aeneas sits down for a moment to relax.

I was still wondering what exactly to do with the poems – promptly on nine the next morning the chauffeur had delivered a second batch – when Tony Sapphire called to help me with the make-up of the next issue. Most of the time he spent at his beach-chalet at Lagoon West, programming an automatic novel, but he put in a day or two each week on *Wave IX*.

I was checking the internal rhyme chains in an IBM sonnet sequence of Xero Paris's as he arrived. While I held the code chart over the sonnets, checking the rhyme lattices, he picked up the sheets of pink quarto on which Aurora's poems were printed.

'Delicious scent,' he commented, fanning the sheets through the air. 'One way to get round an editor.' He started to read the first of the poems, then frowned and put it down.

'Extraordinary. What are they?'

'I'm not altogether sure,' I admitted. 'Echoes in a stone garden.'

Tony read the signature at the bottom of the sheets. ' "Aurora Day." A new subscriber, I suppose. She probably thinks *Wave IX* is the *VT Times*. But what is all this – "nor psalms, nor canticles, nor hollow register to praise the queen of night –"?' He shook his head. 'What are they supposed to be?'

I smiled at him. Like most other writers and poets, he had spent so long sitting in front of his VT set that he had forgotten the period when poetry was actually handspun.

'They're poems, of a sort, obviously.'

'Do you mean she wrote these herself?'

I nodded. 'It has been done that way. In fact the method enjoyed quite a vogue for twenty or thirty centuries. Shakespeare tried it, Milton, Keats and Shelley – it worked reasonably well then.'

'But not now,' Tony said. 'Not since the VT set. How can you compete with an IBM heavy-duty logomatic analogue? Look at this one, for heaven's sake. It sounds like T. S. Eliot. She can't be serious.'

'You may be right. Perhaps the girl's pulling my leg.'

'Girl. She's probably sixty and tipples her eau de cologne. Sad. In some insane way they may mean something.'

'Hold on,' I told him. I was pasting down one of the Xero's satirical pastiches of Rupert Brooke and was six lines short. I handed Tony the master tape and he played it into the IBM, set the metre, rhyme scheme, verbal pairs, and then switched on, waited for the tape to chunter out of the delivery head, tore off six lines and passed them back to me. I didn't even need to read them.

For the next two hours we worked hard. At dusk we had completed over one thousand lines and broke off for a well-earned drink. We moved on to the terrace and sat in the cool evening light, watching the colours melting across the desert, listening to the sand-rays cry in the darkness by Aurora's villa.

'What are all these streamers lying around under here?' Tony asked. He pulled one towards him, caught the strands as they broke in his hand and steered them on to the glass-topped table.

'"– nor canticles, nor hollow register –"' He read the line out, then released the tissue and let it blow away on the wind.

He peered across the shadow-covered dunes at Studio 5. As usual a single light was burning in one of the upper rooms, illuminating the threads unravelling in the sand as they moved towards us.

Tony nodded. 'So that's where she lives.' He picked up another of the streamers that had coiled itself through the railing and was fluttering instantly at his elbow.

'You know, old sport, you're quite literally under siege.'

I was. During the next days a ceaseless bombardment of ever more obscure and bizarre poems reached me, always in two instalments, the first brought by the chauffeur promptly at nine o'clock each morning, the second that evening when the streamers began to blow across the dusk to me. The fragments of Shakespeare and Pound had gone now, and the streamers carried fragmented versions of the poems delivered earlier in the day, almost as if they represented her working drafts. Examining the tapes carefully I realized that, as Aurora Day had said, they were not produced by a VT set. The strands were too delicate to have passed through the spools and high-speed cams of a computer mechanism, and the lettering along them had not been printed but embossed by some process I was unable to identify.

Each day I read the latest offerings, carefully filed them away in the centre drawer of my desk. Finally, when I had a week's production stacked together, I placed them in a return envelope, addressed it 'Aurora Day, Studio 5, The Stars, Vermilion Sands,' and penned a tactful rejection note, suggesting that she would feel ultimately more satisfied if her work appeared in another of the wide range of poetry reviews.

That night I had the first of what was to be a series of highly unpleasant dreams.

Making myself some strong coffee the next morning, I waited blearily for my mind to clear. I went on to the terrace, wondering what had prompted the savage nightmare that had plagued me through the night. The dream had been the first of any kind I had had for several years – one of the pleasant features of beach fatigue is a heavy dreamless sleep, and the sudden irruption of a dream-filled night made me wonder whether Aurora Day, and more particularly her insane poems, were beginning to prey on my mind more than I realized.

My headache took a long time to dissipate. I lay back, watching the Day villa, its windows closed and shuttered, awnings retracted, like a sealed crown. Who was she anyway, I asked myself, and what did she really want?

Five minutes later, I saw the Cadillac swing out of the drive and coast down the Stars towards me.

Not another delivery! The woman was tireless. I waited by the front door, met the driver half way down the steps and took from him a wax-sealed envelope.

'Look,' I said to him confidentially. 'I'd hate to discourage an emerging talent, but I think you might well use any influence you have on your mistress and, you know, generally...' I let the idea hang in front of him, and added: 'By the way, all these streamers that keep blowing across here are getting to be a damn nuisance.'

The chauffeur regarded me out of his red-rimmed foxy eyes, his beaked face contorted in a monstrous grin. Shaking his head sadly, he hobbled back to the car.

As he drove off I opened the letter. Inside was a single sheet of paper.

Mr Ransom,

Your rejection of my poems astounds me. I seriously advise you to reconsider your decision. This is no trifling matter. I expect to see the poems printed in your next issue.

AURORA DAY

That night I had another insane dream.

The next selection of poems arrived when I was still in bed, trying to massage a little sanity back into my mind. I climbed out of bed and made myself a large Martini, ignoring the envelope jutting through the door like the blade of a paper spear.

When I had steadied myself I slit it open, and scanned the three short poems included.

They were dreadful. Dimly I wondered how to persuade Aurora that the requisite talent was missing. Holding the Martini in one hand and peering at the poems in the other, I ambled on to the terrace and slumped down in one of the chairs.

With a shout I sprang into the air, knocking the glass out of my hand. I had sat down on something large and spongy, the size of a cushion but with uneven bony contours.

Looking down, I saw an enormous dead sand-ray lying in the centre of the seat, its white-tipped sting, still viable, projecting a full inch from its sheath above the cranial crest.

Jaw clamped angrily, I went straight into my study, slapped the three poems into an envelope with a rejection slip and scrawled across it: 'Sorry, entirely unsuitable. Please try other publications.'

Half an hour later I drove down to Vermilion Sands and mailed it myself. As I came back I felt quietly pleased with myself.

That afternoon a colossal boil developed on my right cheek.

Tony Sapphire and Raymond Mayo came round the next morning to commiserate. Both thought I was being pigheaded and pedantic.

'Print one,' Tony told me, sitting down on the foot of the bed.

'I'm damned if I will,' I said. I stared out across the desert at Studio 5. Occasionally a window moved and caught the sunlight but otherwise I had seen nothing of my neighbour.

Tony shrugged. 'All you've got to do is accept one and she'll be satisfied.'

'Are you sure?' I asked cynically. 'This may be only the

beginning. For all we know she may have a dozen epics in the bottom of her suitcase.'

Raymond Mayo wandered over to the window beside me, slipped on his dark glasses and scrutinized the villa. I noticed that he looked even more dapper than usual, dark hair smoothed back, profile adjusted for maximum impact.

'I saw her at the "psycho i" last night,' he mused. 'She had a private balcony upon the mezzanine. Quite extroardinary. They had to stop the floor show twice.' He nodded to himself. 'There's something formless and unstated there, reminded me of Dali's "Cosmogonic Venus". Made me realize how absolutely terrifying all women really are. If I were you I'd do whatever I was told.'

I set my jaw, as far as I could, and shook my head dogmatically. 'Go away. You writers are always pouring scorn on editors, but when things get tough who's the first to break? This is the sort of situation I'm prepared to handle, my whole training and discipline tell me instinctively what to do. That crazy neurotic over there is trying to bewitch me. She thinks she can call down a plague of dead rays, boils and nightmares and I'll surrender my conscience.'

Shaking their heads sadly over my obduracy, Tony and Raymond left me to myself.

Two hours later the boil had subsided as mysteriously as it had appeared. I was beginning to wonder why when a pick-up from The Graphis Press in Vermilion Sands delivered the advance five-hundred of the next issue of *Wave IX*.

I carried the cartons into the lounge, then slit off the wrapping, thinking pleasurably of Aurora Day's promise that she would have her poems published in the next issue. She had failed to realize that I had passed the final pages two days beforehand, and that I could hardly have printed her poems even if I had wanted to.

Opening the pages, I turned to the editorial, another in my series of examinations of the present malaise affecting poetry.

However, in place of the usual half-dozen paragraphs of 10-point type I was astounded to see a single line of 24-point, announcing in italic caps:

*A CALL TO GREATNESS!*

I broke off, hurriedly peered at the cover to make sure Graphis had sent me advance copies of the right journal, then raced rapidly through the pages.

The first poem I recognized immediately. I had rejected it only two days earlier. The next three I had also seen and rejected, then came a series that were new to me, all signed 'Aurora Day' and taking the place of the poems I had passed in page proof.

The entire issue had been pirated! Not a single one of the original poems remained, and a completely new make-up had been substituted. I ran back into the lounge and opened a dozen copies. They were all the same.

Ten minutes later I had carried the three cartons out to the incinerator, tipped them in and soaked the copies with petrol, then tossed a match into the centre of the pyre. Simultaneously, a few miles away Graphis Press were doing the same to the remainder of the 5,000 imprint. How the misprinting had occurred they could not explain. They searched out the copy, all on Aurora's typed notepaper, but with editorial markings in my handwriting! My own copy had disappeared, and they soon denied they had ever received it.

As the heavy flames beat into the hot sunlight I thought that through the thick brown smoke I could see a sudden burst of activity coming from my neighbour's house. Windows were opening under the awnings, and the hunchbacked figure of the chauffeur was scurrying along the terrace.

Standing on the roof, her white gown billowing around her like an enormous silver fleece, Aurora Day looked down at me.

Whether it was the large quantity of Martini I had drunk that morning, the recent boil on my cheek or the fumes from the burning petrol, I'm not sure, but as I walked back into the house I felt unsteady, and sat down hazily on the top step, closing my eyes as my brain swam.

After a few seconds my head cleared again. Leaning on my knees, I focused my eyes on the blue glass step between my feet. Cut into the surface in neat letters was:

*Why so pale and wan, fond lover?*
*Prithee, why so pale?*

Still too weak to more than register an automatic protest against this act of vandalism, I pulled myself to my feet, taking the door key out of my dressing-gown pocket. As I inserted it into the lock I noticed, inscribed into the brass seat of the lock:

*Turn the key deftly in the oiled wards.*

There were other inscriptions all over the black leather panelling of the door, cut in the same neat script, the lines crossing each other at random, like filigree decoration around a baroque salver.

Closing the door behind me, I walked into the lounge. The walls seemed darker than usual, and I realized that their entire surface was covered with row upon row of finely cut lettering, endless fragments of verse stretching from ceiling to fioor.

I picked my glass off the table and raised it to my lips. The blue crystal bowl had been embossed with the same copperplate lines, spiralling down the stem to the base.

*Drink to me only with thine eyes.*

Everything in the lounge was covered with the same fragments – the desk, lampstands and shades, the bookshelves, the keys of the baby grand, even the lip of the record on the stereogram turntable.

Dazed, I raised my hand to my face, in horror saw that the surface of my skin was interlaced by a thousand tattoos, writhing and coiling across my hands and arms like insane serpents.

Dropping my glass, I ran to the mirror over the fireplace, saw my face covered with the same tattooing, a living manuscript in which the ink still ran, the letters running and changing as if the pen still cast them.

*You spotted snakes with double tongue . . .*
*Weaving spiders, come not here.*

I flung myself away from the mirror, ran out on to the terrace, my feet slipping in the piles of coloured streamers which the evening wind was carrying over the balcony, then vaulted down over the railing on to the ground below.

I covered the distance between our villas in a few moments, raced up the darkening drive to the black front door. It opened as my hand reached for the bell, and I plunged through into the crystal hallway.

Aurora Day was waiting for me on the chaise longue by the fountain pool, feeding the ancient white fish that clustered around her. As I stepped across to her she smiled quietly to the fish and whispered to them.

'Aurora!' I cried. 'For heaven's sake, I give in! Take anything you want, anything, but leave me alone!'

For a moment she ignored me and went on quietly feeding the fish. Suddenly a thought of terror plunged through my mind. Were the huge white carp now nestling at her fingers once her lovers?

We sat together in the luminescent dusk, the long shadows playing across the purple landscape of Dali's 'Persistence of

Memory' on the wall behind Aurora, the fish circling slowly in the fountain beside us.

She had stated her terms: nothing less than absolute control of the magazine, freedom to impose her own policy, to make her own selection of material. Nothing would be printed without her first approval.

'Don't worry,' she had said lightly. 'Our agreement will apply to one issue only.' Amazingly she showed no wish to publish her own poems – the pirated issue had merely been a device to bring me finally to surrender.

'Do you think one issue will be enough?' I asked, wondering what really she would do with it now.

She looked up at me idly, tracing patterns across the surface of the pool with a green-tipped finger. 'It all depends on you and your companions. When will you come to your senses and become poets again?'

I watched the patterns in the pool. In some miraculous way they remained etched across the surface.

In the hours, like millennia, we had sat together I seemed to have told her everything about myself, yet learned almost nothing about Aurora. One thing alone was clear – her obsession with the art of poetry. In some curious way she regarded herself as personally responsible for the present ebb at which it found itself, but her only remedy seemed completely retrogressive.

'You must come and meet my friends at the colony,' I suggested.

'I will,' she said. 'I hope I can help them. They all have so much to learn.'

I smiled at this. 'I'm afraid you won't find them very sympathetic to that view. Most of them regard themselves as virtuosos. For them the quest for the perfect sonnet ended years ago. The computer produces nothing else.'

Aurora scoffed. 'They're not poets but mere mechanics. Look at these collections of so-called verse. Three poems and sixty pages of operating instructions. Nothing but volts and amps. When I say they have everything to learn, I mean about their own hearts, not about technique; about the soul of music, not its form.'

She paused to stretch herself, her beautiful body uncoiling like a python. She leaned forward and began to speak earnestly. 'Poetry is dead today, not because of these machines, but because poets no longer search for their true inspiration.'

'Which is?'

Aurora shook her head sadly. 'You call yourself a poet and yet you ask me that?'

She stared down at the pool, her eyes listless. For a moment an expression of profound sadness passed across her face, and I realized that she felt some deep sense of guilt or inadequacy, that some failing of her own was responsible for the present malaise. Perhaps it was this sense of inadequacy that made me unafraid of her.

'Have you ever heard the legend of Melander and Corydon?' she asked.

'Vaguely,' I said, casting my mind back. 'Melander was the Muse of Poetry, if I remember. Wasn't Corydon a court poet who killed himself for her?'

'Good,' Aurora told me. 'You're not completely illiterate, after all. Yes, the court poets found that they had lost their inspiration and that their ladies were spurning them for the company of the knights, so they sought out Melander, the Muse, who told them that she had brought this spell upon them because they had taken their art for granted, forgetting the source from whom it really came. They protested that of course they thought of her always – a blatant lie – but she refused to believe them and told them that they would not recover their power until one of them sacrificed his life for her. Naturally none of them would do so, with the exception of a young poet of great talent called Corydon, who loved the goddess and was the only one to retain his power. For the other poets' sake he killed himself...'

'... to Melander's undying sorrow,' I concluded. 'She was not expecting him to give his life for his art. A beautiful myth,' I agreed. 'But I'm afraid you'll find no Corydons here.'

'I wonder,' Aurora said softly. She stirred the water in the pool, the broken surface throwing a ripple of light across the walls and ceiling. Then I saw that a long series of friezes ran around the lounge depicting the very legend Aurora had been describing. The first panel, on my extreme left, showed the poets and troubadours gathered around the goddess, a tall white-gowned figure whose face bore a remarkable resemblance to Aurora's. As I traced the story through the successive panels the likeness became even more marked, and I assumed that she had sat as Melander for the artist. Had she, in some way, identified herself with the goddess in the myth? In which case, who was her Corydon? – perhaps the artist himself. I searched the panels for the suicidal poet, a slim blond-maned youth whose face, although slightly familiar, I could not identify. However, behind the principal figures in all the scenes I certainly recognized another, her faun-faced chauffeur, here with ass's legs and wild woodwind, representing none other than the attendant Pan.

I had almost detected another likeness among the figures in the friezes when Aurora noticed me searching the panels. She stopped stirring the pool. As the ripples subsided the panels sank again into darkness. For a few seconds Aurora stared at me as if she had forgotten who I was. She appeared to have become tired and withdrawn, as if recapitulating the myth had evoked private memories of pain and fatigue. Simultaneously the hallway and glass-enclosed portico seemed to grow dark and sombre, reflecting her own darkening mood, so dominant was her presence that the air itself paled as she did. Again I felt that her world, into which I had stepped, was completely compounded of illusion.

She was asleep. Around her the room was almost in darkness. The pool lights had faded, the crystal columns that had shone around us were dull and extinguished, like trunks of opaque glass. The only light came from the flower-like jewel between her sleeping breasts.

I stood up and walked softly across to her, looked down at her strange face, its skin smooth and grey, like some pharaonic bride in a basalt dream. Then, beside me at the door I noticed the hunched figure of the chauffeur. His peaked cap hid his face, but the two watchful eyes were fixed on me like small coals.

As we left, hundreds of sleeping sand-rays were dotted about the moonlit floor of the desert. We stepped between them and moved away silently in the Cadillac.

When I reached the villa I went straight into the study, ready to start work on assembling the next issue. During the return ride I had quickly decided on the principal cue-themes and key-images which I would play into the VT sets. All programmed for maximum repetition, within twenty-four hours I would have a folio of moon-sick, muse-mad dithyrambs which would stagger Aurora Day by their heartfelt simplicity and inspiration.

As I entered the study my shoe caught on something sharp. I bent down in the darkness, and found a torn strip of computer circuitry embedded in the white leather flooring.

When I switched on the light I saw that someone had smashed the three VT sets, pounding them to a twisted pulp in a savage excess of violence.

Mine had not been the only targets. Next morning, as I sat at my desk contemplating the three wrecked computers, the telephone rang with news of similar outrages all the way down the Stars. Tony Sapphire's 50-watt IBM had been hammered to pieces, and Raymond Mayo's four new Philco Versomatics had been smashed beyond hope of repair. As far as I could gather, not a single VT set had been left untouched. The previous evening, between the hours of six and midnight, someone had moved rapidly down the Stars, slipped into the studios and apartments and singlemindedly wrecked every VT set.

I had a good idea who. As I climbed out of the Cadillac on my return from Aurora I had noticed two heavy wrenches on the seat beside the chauffeur. However, I decided not to call the police and prefer charges. For one thing, the problem of filling *Wave IX* now looked almost insoluble. When I telephoned Graphis Press I found, more or less as expected, that all Aurora's copy had been mysteriously mislaid.

The problem remained – what would I put in the issue? I couldn't afford to miss an edition or my subscribers would fade away like ghosts.

I telephoned Aurora and pointed this out.

'We should go to press again within a week, otherwise our contract expires and I'll never get another. And reimbursing a year's advance subscriptions would bankrupt me. We've simply got to find some copy. As the new managing editor have you any suggestions?'

Aurora chuckled. 'I suppose you're thinking that I might mysteriously reassemble all those smashed machines?'

'It's an idea,' I agreed, waving at Tony Sapphire who had just called in. 'Otherwise I'm afraid we're never going to get any copy.'

'I can't understand you,' Aurora replied: 'Surely there's one very simple method.'

'Is there? What's that?'

'Write some yourself!'

Before I could protest she burst into a peal of high laughter. 'I gather there are some twenty-three able-bodied versifiers and so-called poets in Vermilion Sands' – this was exactly the number of places broken into the previous evening – 'well, let's see some of them versify.'

'Aurora!' I snapped. 'You can't be serious. Listen, for heaven's sake, this is no joking –'

But she had put the phone down. I turned to Tony Sapphire, then sat back limply and contemplated an intact tape spool I had recovered from one of the sets. 'It looks as if I've had it. Did you hear that – "Write some yourself"?'

'She must be insane,' Tony agreed.

'It's all part of this tragic obsession of hers,' I explained, lowering my voice. 'She genuinely believes she's the Muse of Poetry, returned to earth to re-inspire the dying race of poets. Last night she referred to the myth of Melander and Corydon. I think she's seriously waiting for some young poet to give his life for her.'

Tony nodded. 'She's missing the point, though. Fifty years ago a few people wrote poetry, but no one read it. Now no one writes it either. The VT set merely simplifies the whole process.'

I agreed with him, but of course Tony was somewhat prejudiced there, being one of those people who believed that literature was in essence both unreadable and unwritable. The automatic novel he had been "writing" was over ten million words long, intended to be one of those gigantic grotesques that tower over the highways of literary history, terrifying the unwary traveller. Unfortunately he had never bothered to get it printed, and the memory drum which carried the electronic coding had been wrecked in the previous night's pogrom.

I was equally annoyed. One of my VT sets had been steadily producing a transliteration of James Joyce's *Ulysses* in terms of a Hellenic Greek setting, a pleasant academic exercise which would have provided an objective test of Joyce's masterpiece by the degree of exactness with which the transliteration matched the original Odyssey. This too had been destroyed.

We watched Studio 5 in the bright morning light. The cerise

Cadillac had disappeared somewhere, so presumably Aurora was driving around Vermilion Sands, astounding the café crowds.

I picked up the terrace telephone and sat on the rail. 'I suppose I might as well call everyone up and see what they can do.'

I dialled the first number.

Raymond Mayo said: 'Write some myself? Paul, you're insane.'

Xero Paris said: 'Myself? Of course, Paul, with my toes.'

Fairchild de Mille said: 'It would be rather chic, but...'

Kurt Butterworth said, sourly: 'Ever tried to? How?'

Marlene McClintic said: 'Darling, I wouldn't dare. It might develop the wrong muscles or something.'

Sigismund Lutitsch said. 'No, no. Siggy now in new zone. Electronic sculpture, plasma in super-cosmic collisions. Listen –'

Robin Saunders, Macmillan Freebody and Angel Petit said: 'No.'

Tony brought me a drink and I pressed on down the list. 'It's no good,' I said at last. 'No one writes verse any more. Let's face it. After all, do you or I?'

Tony pointed to the notebook. 'There's one name left – we might as well sweep the decks clean before we take off for Red Beach.'

'Tristram Caldwell,' I read. 'That's the shy young fellow with the footballer's build. Something is always wrong with his set. Might as well try him.'

A soft honey-voiced girl answered the phone.

'Tristram?' she purred. 'Er, yes, I think he's here.'

There were sounds of wrestling around on a bed, during which the telephone bounced on the floor a few times, and then Caldwell answered.

'Hello, Ransom, what can I do for you?'

'Tristram,' I said, 'I take it you were paid the usual surprise call last night. Or didn't you notice? How's your VT set?'

'VT set?' he repeated. 'It's fine, just fine.'

'What?' I shouted. 'You mean yours is undamaged? Tristram, pull yourself together and listen to me!' Quickly I explained our problem, but Tristram suddenly began to laugh.

'Well, I think that's just damn funny, don't you? Really rich. I think she's right. Let's get back to the old crafts –'

'Never mind the old crafts,' I told him irritably. 'All I'm interested in is getting some copy together for the next issue. If your set is working we're saved.'

'Well there, wait a minute, Paul. I've been slightly preoccupied recently, haven't had a chance to see the set.'

I waited while he wandered off. From the sounds of his footsteps and an impatient shout of the girl's, to which he replied distantly, it seemed he had gone outside into the yard. A door slammed open somewhere and there was a vague rummaging. A curious place to keep a VT set, I thought. Then there was a loud hammering noise.

Finally Tristram picked up the phone again. 'Sorry, Paul, but it looks as if she paid me a visit too. The set's a total wreck.' He paused while I cursed the air, then said: 'Look, though, is she really serious about the hand-made material? I take it that's what you were calling about?'

'Yes,' I told him. 'Believe me, I'll print anything. It has to get past Aurora, though. Have you got any old copy lying around?'

Tristram chuckled again. 'You know, Paul, old boy, I believe I have. Rather despaired of ever getting it into print but I'm glad now I held on to it. Tell you what, I'll tidy it up and let you have it tomorrow. Few sonnets, a ballad or two, you should find it interesting.'

He was right. Five minutes after I opened his parcel the next morning I knew he was trying to fool us.

'This is the same old thing,' I explained to Tony. 'That cunning Adonis. Look at these assonances and feminine rhymes, the drifting caesura – the unmistakable Caldwell signature, worn tapes on the rectifier circuits and a leaking condenser. I've been having to re-tread these for years to smooth them out. He's got his set there working away after all.'

'What are you going to do?' Tony asked. 'He'll just deny it.'

'Obviously. Anyway, I can use the material. Who cares if the whole issue is by Tristram Caldwell.'

I started to slip the pages into an envelope before taking them round to Aurora, when an idea occurred to me.

'Tony, I've just had another of my brilliancies. The perfect method of curing this witch of her obsession and exacting sweet revenge at the same time. Suppose we play along with Tristram and tell Aurora that these poems were hand-written by him. His style is thoroughly retrograde and his themes are everything Aurora could ask for – listen to these – "Homage to Cleo," "Minerva 231," "Silence becomes Electra." She'll pass them for press, we'll print this weekend and then, lo and behond, we reveal that these poems apparently born out of the burning breast of Tristram Caldwell are nothing more than a collection of cliché-ridden transcripts from a derelict VT set, the worst possible automatic maunderings.'

Tony whooped. 'Tremendous! She'd never live it down. But do you think she'll be taken in?'

'Why not? Haven't you realized that she sincerely expects us all to sit down and produce a series of model classical exercises on "Night and Day", "Summer and Winter", and so on. When only Caldwell produces anything she'll be only too glad to give him her imprimatur. Remember, our agreement only refers to this issue, and the onus is on her. She's got to find material somewhere.'

So we launched our scheme. All afternoon I pestered Tristram, telling him that Aurora had adored his first consignment and was eager to see more. Duly the next day a second batch arrived, all, as luck would have it, in longhand, although remarkably faded for material fresh from his VT set the previous day. However, I was only too glad for anything that would reinforce the illusion. Aurora was more and more pleased, and showed no suspicions whatever. Here and there she made a minor criticism but refused to have anything altered or rewritten.

'But we always rewrite. Aurora,' I told her. 'One can't expect an infallible selection of images. The number of synonyms is too great.' Wondering whether I had gone too far, I added hastily: 'It doesn't matter whether the author is man or robot, the principle is the same.'

'Really?' Aurora said archly. 'However, I think we'll leave these just as Mr Caldwell wrote them.'

I didn't bother to point out the hopeless fallacy in her attitude, and merely collected the initialled manuscripts and hurried home with them. Tony was at my desk, deep in the phone, pumping Tristram for more copy.

He capped the mouthpiece and gestured to me. 'He's playing coy, probably trying to raise us to two cents a thousand. Pretends he's out of material. Is it worth calling his bluff?'

I shook my head. 'Dangerous. If Aurora discovers we're involved in this fraud of Tristram's she might do anything. Let me talk to him.' I took the phone. 'What's the matter Tristram, production's way down. We need more material, old boy. Shorten the line, why are you wasting tapes with all these alexandrines?'

'Ransom, what the hell are you talking about? I'm not a damned factory, I'm a poet, I write when I have something to say in the only suitable way to say it.'

'Yes, yes,' I rejoined, 'but I have fifty pages to fill and only a few days in which to do it. You've given me about ten so you've just got to keep up the flow. What have you produced today?'

'Well, I'm working on another sonnet, some nice things in it – to Aurora herself, as a matter of fact.'

'Great,' I told him, 'but careful with those vocabulary selectors. Remember the golden rule: the ideal sentence is one word long. What else have you got?'

'What else? Nothing. This is likely to take all week, perhaps all year.'

I nearly swallowed the phone. 'Tristram, what's the matter? For heaven's sake, haven't you paid the power bill or something? Have they cut you off?'

Before I could find out, however, he had rung off.

'One sonnet a day,' I said to Tony. 'Good God, he must be on manual. Crazy idiot, he probably doesn't realize how complicated those circuits are.'

We sat tight and waited. Nothing came the next morning, and nothing the morning after that. Luckily, however, Aurora wasn't in the least surprised; in fact, if anything she was pleased that Tristram's rate of progress was slowing.

'One poem is enough,' she told me, 'a complete statement. Nothing more needs to be said, an interval of eternity closes for ever.'

Reflectively, she straightened the petals of a hyacinth. 'Perhaps he needs a little encouragement,' she decided.

I could see she wanted to meet him.

'Why don't you ask him over for dinner?' I suggested.

She brightened immediately. 'I will.' She picked up the telephone and handed it to me.

As I dialled Tristram's number I felt a sudden pang of envy and disappointment. Around me the friezes told the story of Melander and Corydon, but I was too preoccupied to anticipate the tragedy the next week would bring.

During the days that followed Tristram and Aurora Day were always together. In the morning they would usually drive out to the film sets at Lagoon West, the chauffeur at the wheel of the huge Cadillac. In the evenings, as I sat out alone on the terrace, watching the lights of Studio 5 shine out into the warm darkness, I could hear their fragmented voices carried across the sand, the faint sounds of crystal music.

I would like to think that I resented their relationship, but to be truthful I cared very little after the initial disappointment had worn off. The beach fatigue from which I suffered numbed the senses insidiously, blunting despair and hope alike.

When, three days after their first meeting, Aurora and Tristram suggested that we all go ray-fishing at Lagoon West, I accepted gladly, eager to observe their affair at closer quarters.

As we set off down the Stars there was no hint of what was to come. Tristram and Aurora were together in the Cadillac while Tony Sapphire, Raymond Mayo and I brought up the rear in Tony's Chevrolet. We could see them through the blue rear window of the Cadillac, Tristram reading the sonnet to Aurora which he had just completed. When we climbed out of the cars at Lagoon West and made our way over to the old abstract film sets near the sand reefs, they were walking hand in hand. Tristram in his white beach shoes and suit looked very much like an Edwardian dandy at a boating party.

The chauffeur carried the picnic hampers, and Raymond Mayo and Tony the spear-guns and nets. Down the reefs below we could see the rays nesting by the thousands, scores of double mambas sleek with off-season hibernation.

After we had settled ourselves under the awnings Raymond and Tristram decided on the course and then gathered everyone together. Strung out in a loose line we began to make our way down into one of the reefs, Aurora on Tristram's arm.

'Ever done any ray-fishing?' Tristram asked me as we entered one of the lower galleries.

'Never,' I said. 'I'll just watch this time. I hear you're quite an expert.'

'Well, with luck I won't be killed.' He pointed to the rays clinging to the cornices above us, wheeling up into the sky as we approached, whistling and screeching. In the dim light the white tips of their stings flexed in their sheaths. 'Unless they're really frightened they'll stay well away from you,' he told us. 'The art is to prevent them from becoming frightened, select one and approach it so slowly that it sits staring at you until you're close enough to shoot it.'

Raymond Mayo had found a large purple mamba resting in a narrow crevice about ten yards on our right. He moved up to it quietly, watching the sting protrude from its sheath and weave menacingly, waiting just long enough for it to retract, lulling the ray with a low humming sound. Finally, when he was five feet away, he raised the gun and took careful aim.

'There may seem little to it,' Tristram whispered to Aurora and me, 'but in fact he's completely at the ray's mercy now. If it chose to attack he'd be defenceless.' The bolt snapped from Raymond's gun and struck the ray on its spinal crest, stunning it instantly. Quickly he stepped over and scooped it into the net, where it revived after a few seconds, threshed its black triangular wings helplessly and then lay inertly.

We moved through the groins and galleries, the sky a narrow winding interval overhead, following the pathways that curved down into the bed of the reef. Now and then the wheeling rays rising out of our way would brush against the reef and drifts of fine sand would cascade over us. Raymond and Tristram shot several more rays, leaving the chauffeur to carry the nets. Gradually our party split into two, Tony and Raymond taking one pathway with the chauffeur, while I stayed with Aurora and Tristram.

As we moved along I noticed that Aurora's face had become less relaxed, her movements slightly more deliberate and controlled. I had the impression she was watching Tristram carefully, glancing sideways at him as she held his arm.

We entered the terminal fornix of the reef, a deep cathedral-like chamber from which a score of galleries spiralled off to surface like the arms of a galaxy. In the darkness around us the thousands of rays hung motionlessly, their phosphorescing stings flexing and retracting like winking stars.

Two hundred feet away, on the far side of the chamber, Raymond Mayo and the chauffeur emerged from one of the galleries. They waited there for a few moments. Suddenly I heard Tony shouting out. Raymond dropped his spear-gun and disappeared into the gallery.

Excusing myself, I ran across the chamber. I found them in the narrow corridor, peering around in the darkness.

'I tell you,' Tony was insisting. 'I heard the damn thing singing.'

'Impossible,' Raymond told him. They argued with each other, then gave up the search for the mysterious song-ray and stepped down into the chamber. As we went I thought I saw the chauffeur replace something in his pocket. With his beaked face and insane eyes, his hunched figure hung about with the nets of writhing rays, he looked like a figure from Hieronymus Bosch.

After exchanging a few words with Raymond and Tony I turned to make my way back to the others, but they had left the chamber. Wondering which of the galleries they had chosen, I stepped a few yards into the mouth of each one, finally saw them on one of the ramps curving away above me.

I was about to retrace my steps and join them when I caught a glimpse of Aurora's face in profile, saw once again her expression of watchful intent. Changing my mind, I moved quietly along the spiral, just below them, the falls of sand masking my footsteps, keeping them in view through the intervals between the overhanging columns.

At one point I was only a few yards from them, and heard Aurora say clearly: 'Isn't there a theory that you can trap rays by singing to them?'

'By mesmerizing them?' Tristram asked. 'Let's try.'

They moved farther away, and Aurora's voice sounded out softly, a low crooning tone. Gradually the sound rose, echoing and re-echoing through the high vaults, the rays stirring in the darkness.

As we neared the surface their numbers grew, and Aurora stopped and guided Tristram towards a narrow sun-filled arena, bounded by hundred-foot walls, open to the sky above.

Unable to see them now, I retreated into the gallery and climbed the inner slope on to the next level, and from there on to the stage above. I made my way to the edge of the gallery, from which I could now easily observe the arena below. As I did so, however, I was aware of an eerie and penetrating noise, at once toneless and all-pervading, which filled the entire reef, like the high-pitched sounds perceived by epileptics before a seizure. Down in the arena Tristram was searching the walls, trying to identify the source of the noise, hands raised to his head. He had taken his eyes off Aurora, who was standing behind him, arms motionless at her sides, palms slightly raised, like an entranced medium.

Fascinated by this curious stance, I was abruptly distracted by a terrified screeching that came from the lower levels of the reef. It was accompanied by a confused leathery flapping, and almost immediately a cloud of flying rays, frantically trying to escape from the reef, burst from the galleries below.

As they turned into the arena, sweeping low over the heads of Tristram and Aurora, they seemed to lose their sense of direction, and within a moment the arena was packed by a swarm of circling rays, all diving about uncertainly.

Screaming in terror at the rays whipping past her face, Aurora emerged from her trance. Tristram had taken off his straw hat and was striking furiously at them, shielding Aurora with his other arm. Together they backed towards a narrow fault in the rear wall of the arena, which provided an escape route into the galleries on the far side. Following this route to the edge of the cliffs above, I was surprised to see the squat figure of the chauffeur, now divested of his nets and gear, peering down at the couple below.

By now the hundreds of rays jostling within the arena almost obscured Tristram and Aurora. She reappeared from the narrow fault, shaking her head desperately. Their escape route was sealed! Quickly Tristram motioned her to her knees, then leapt into the middle of the arena, slapping wildly at the rays with his hat, trying to drive them away from Aurora.

For a few seconds he was successful. Like a cloud of giant hornets the rays wheeled off in disorder. Horrified, I watched them descend upon him again. Before I could shout Tristram had fallen. The rays swooped and hovered over his outstretched body, then swirled away, soaring into the sky, apparently released from the vortex.

Tristram lay face downwards, his blond hair spilled across the sand, arms twisted loosely. I stared at his body, amazed by the swiftness with which he had died, and looked across to Aurora.

She too was watching the body, but with an expression that showed neither pity nor terror. Gathering her skirt in one hand, she turned and slipped away through the fault –

The escape route had been open after all! Astonished, I realized that Aurora had deliberately told Tristram that the route was closed, virtually forcing him to attack the rays.

A minute later she emerged from the mouth of the gallery above. Briefly she peered down into the arena, the black-uniformed chauffeur at her elbow, watching the motionless body of Tristram. Then they hurried away.

Racing after them, I began to shout at the top of my voice, hoping to attract Tony and Raymond Mayo. As I reached the mouth of the reef my voice boomed and echoed into the galleries below. A hundred yards away Aurora and the chauffeur were stepping into the Cadillac. With a roar of exhaust it swung away among the sets, sending up clouds of dust that obscured the enormous abstract patterns.

I ran towards Tony's car. By the time I reached it the Cadillac was half a mile away, burning across the desert like an escaping dragon.

That was the last I saw of Aurora Day. I managed to follow them as far as the highway to Lagoon West, but there, on the open road, the big car left me behind, and ten miles farther on, by the time I reached Lagoon West, I had lost them completely. At one of the gas stations where the highway forks to Vermilion Sands and Red Beach I asked if anyone had seen a cerise Cadillac go by. Two attendants said they had, on the road *towards* me, and although they both swore this, I suppose Aurora's magic must have confused them.

I decided to try her villa and took the fork back to Vermilion Sands, cursing myself for not anticipating what had happened. I, ostensibly a poet, had failed to take another poet's dreams seriously. Aurora had explicitly forecast Tristram's death.

Studio 5, The Stars, was silent and empty. The rays had gone from the drive, and the black glass door was wide open, the remains of a few streamers drifting across the dust that gathered on the floor. The hallway and lounge were in darkness, and only the white carp in the pool provided a glimmer of light. The air was still and unbroken, as if the house had been empty for centuries.

Cursorily I ran my eye round the friezes in the lounge, then saw that I knew all the faces of the figures in the panels. The likenesses were almost photographic. Tristram was Corydon, Aurora Melander, the chauffeur the god Pan. And I saw myself, Tony Sapphire, Raymond Mayo, Fairchild de Mille and the other members of the colony.

Leaving the friezes, I made my way past the pool. It was now evening, and through the open doorway were the distant lights of Vermilion Sands, the headlights sweeping along the Stars reflected in the glass roof-tiles of my villa. A light wind had risen, stirring the streamers, and as I went down the steps a gust of air moved through the house and caught the door, slamming it behind me. The loud report boomed through the house, a concluding statement upon the whole sequence of fantasy and disaster, a final notice of the departure of the enchantress.

As I walked back across the desert and last streamers were moving over the dark sand, I strode firmly through them, trying to reassemble my own reality again. The fragments of Aurora Day's insane poems caught the dying desert light as they dissolved about my feet, the fading debris of a dream.

Reaching the villa, I saw that the lights were on. I raced inside and to my astonishment discovered the blond figure of Tristram stretched out lazily in a chair on the terrace, an ice-filled glass in one hand.

He eyed me genially, winked broadly before I could speak and put a forefinger to his lips.

I stepped over to him. 'Tristram,' I whispered hoarsely. 'I thought you were dead. What on earth happened down there?'

He smiled at me. 'Sorry, Paul, I had a hunch you were watching. Aurora got away, didn't she?'

I nodded. 'Their car was too fast for the Chevrolet. But weren't you hit by one of the rays? I saw you fall, I thought you'd been killed outright.'

'So did Aurora. Neither of you know much about rays, do you? Their stings are passive in the on season, old chap, or nobody would be allowed in there.' He grinned at me. 'Ever hear of the myth of Melander and Corydon?'

I sat down weakly on the seat next to him. In two minutes

he explained what had happened. Aurora had told him of the myth, and partly out of sympathy for her, and partly for amusement, he had decided to play out his role. All the while he had been describing the danger and viciousness of the rays he had been egging Aurora on deliberately, and had provided her with a perfect opportunity to stage his sacrificial murder.

'It *was* murder, of course,' I told him. 'Believe me, I saw the glint in her eye. She really wanted you killed.'

Tristram shrugged. 'Don't look so shocked, old boy. After all, poetry is a serious business.'

Raymond and Tony Sapphire knew nothing of what had happened. Tristram had put together a story of how Aurora had suffered a sudden attack of claustrophobia, and rushed off in a frenzy.

'I wonder what Aurora will do now,' Tristram mused. 'Her prophecy's been fulfilled. Perhaps she'll feel more confident of her own beauty. You know, she had a colossal sense of physical inadequacy. Like the original Melander, who was surprised when Corydon killed himself, Aurora confused her art with her own person.'

I nodded. 'I hope she isn't too disappointed when she finds poetry is still being written in the bad old way. That reminds me, I've got twenty-five pages to fill. How's your VT set running?'

'No longer have one. Wrecked it the morning you phoned up. Haven't used the thing for years.'

I sat up. 'Do you mean that those sonnets you've been sending in are all hand-written?'

'Absolutely, old boy. Every single one a soul-grafted gem.'

I lay back groaning. 'God, I was relying on your set to save me. What the hell am I going to do?'

Tristram grinned. 'Start writing it yourself. Remember the prophecy. Perhaps it will come true. After all, Aurora thinks I'm dead.'

I cursed him roundly. 'If it's any help, I wish you were. Do you know what this is going to cost me?'

After he had gone I went into the study and added up what copy I had left, found that there were exactly twenty-three pages to fill. Oddly enough that represented one page for each of the registered poets at Vermilion Sands. Except that none of them, apart from Tristram, was capable of producing a single line.

It was midnight, but the problems facing the magazine would take every minute of the next twenty-four hours, when the final deadline expired. I had almost decided to write something myself when the telephone rang. At first I thought it was Aurora Day – the voice was high and feminine – but it was only Fairchild de Mille.

'What are you doing up so late?' I growled at him. 'Shouldn't you be getting your beauty sleep?'

'Well, I suppose I should, Paul, but do you know a rather incredible thing happened to me this evening. Tell me, are you still looking for original hand-written verse? I started writing something a couple of hours ago, it's not bad really. About Aurora Day, as a matter of fact. I think you'll like it.'

Sitting up, I congratulated him fulsomely, noting down the linage.

Five minutes later the telephone rang again. This time it was Angel Petit. He too had a few hand-written verses I might be interested in. Again, dedicated to Aurora Day.

Within the next half hour the telephone rang a score of times. Every poet in Vermilion Sands seemed to be awake. I heard from Macmillan Freebody, Robin Saunders and the rest of them. All, mysteriously that evening, had suddenly felt the urge to write something original, and in a few minutes had tossed off a couple of stanzas to the memory of Aurora Day.

I was musing over it when I stood up after the last call. It was 12.45, and I should have been tired out, but my brain felt keen and alive, a thousand ideas running through it. A phrase formed itself in my mind. I picked up my pad and wrote it down.

Time seemed to dissolve. Within five minutes I had produced the first piece of verse I had written for over ten years. Behind it a dozen more poems lay just below the surface of my mind, waiting like gold in a loaded vein to be brought out into daylight.

Sleep would wait. I reached for another sheet of paper and then noticed a letter on the desk to the IBM agency in Red Beach, enclosing an order for three new VT sets.

Smiling to myself, I tore it into a dozen pieces.

# The Thousand Dreams of Stellavista

No one ever comes to Vermilion Sands now, and I suppose there are few people who have ever heard of it. But ten years ago, when Fay and I first went to live at 99 Stellavista, just before our marriage broke up, the colony was still remembered as the one-time playground of movie stars, delinquent heiresses and eccentric cosmopolites in those fabulous years before the Recess. Admittedly most of the abstract villas and fake palazzos were empty, their huge gardens overgrown, two-level swimming pools long drained, and the whole place was degenerating like an abandoned amusement park, but there was enough bizarre extravagance in the air to make one realize that the giants had only just departed.

I remember the day we first drove down Stellavista in the property agent's car, and how exhilarated Fay and I were, despite our bogus front of bourgeois respectability. Fay, I think, was even a little awed – one or two of the big names were living on behind the shuttered terraces – and we must have been the easiest prospects the young agent had seen for months.

Presumably this was why he tried to work off the really weird places first. The half dozen we saw to begin with were obviously the old regulars, faithfully paraded in the hope that some unwary client might be staggered into buying one of them, or failing that, temporarily lose all standards of comparison and take the first tolerably conventional pile to come along.

One, just off Stellavista and M, would have shaken even an old-guard surrealist on a heroin swing. Screened from the road by a mass of dusty rhododendrons, it consisted of six aluminium-shelled spheres suspended like the elements of a mobile from an enormous concrete davit. The largest sphere contained the lounge, the others, successively smaller and spiralling upwards into the air, the bedrooms and kitchen. Many of the hull plates had been holed, and the entire slightly tarnished structure hung down into the weeds poking through the cracked concrete court like a collection of forgotten spaceships in a vacant lot.

Stamers, the agent, left us sitting in the car, partly shielded by the rhododendrons. He ran across to the entrance and switched the place on (all the houses in Vermilion Sands, it goes without saying, were psychotropic). There was a dim whirring, and the spheres tipped and began to rotate, brushing against the undergrowth.

Fay sat in the car, staring up in amazement at this awful, beautiful thing, but out of curiosity I got out and walked over to the entrance, the main sphere slowing as I approached, uncertainly steering a course towards me, the smaller ones following.

According to the descriptive brochure, the house had been built eight years earlier for a TV mogul as a weekend retreat. The pedigree was a long one, through two movie starlets, a psychiatrist, an ultrasonic composer (the late Dmitri Shochmann – a notorious madman. I remembered that he had invited a score of guests to his suicide party, but no one had turned up to watch. Chagrined, he bungled the attempt.) and an automobile stylist. With such an overlay of more or less blue-chip responses built into it, the house should have been snapped up within a week, even in Vermilion Sands. To have been on the market for several months, if not years, indicated that the previous tenants had been none too happy there.

Ten feet from me, the main sphere hovered uncertainly, the entrance extending downwards. Stamers stood in the open doorway, smiling encouragingly, but the house seemed nervous of something. As I stepped forward it suddenly jerked away, almost in alarm, the entrance retracting and sending a low shudder through the rest of the spheres.

It's always interesting to watch a psychotropic house try to adjust itself to strangers, particularly those at all guarded or suspicious. The responses vary, a blend of past reactions to negative emotions, the hostility of the previous tenants, a traumatic encounter with a bailiff or burglar (though both these usually stay well away from PT houses; the dangers of an inverting balcony or the sudden deflatus of a corridor are too great). The initial reaction can be a surer indication of a house's true condition than any amount of sales talk about horsepower and moduli of elasticity.

This one was definitely on the defensive. When I climbed on to the entrance Stamers was fiddling desperately with the control console recessed into the wall behind the door, damping the volume down as low as possible. Usually a property agent will select medium/full, trying to heighten the PT responses.

He smiled thinly at me. 'Circuits are a little worn. Nothing serious, we'll replace them on contract. Some of the previous owners were show-business people, had an over-simplified view of the full life.'

I nodded, walking on to the balcony which ringed the wide sunken lounge. It was a beautiful room all right, with opaque plastex walls and white fluo-glass ceiling, but something terrible had happened there. As it responded to me, the ceiling lifted slightly and the walls grew less opaque, reflecting my perspective-seeking eye. I noticed that curious mottled knots were forming where the room had been strained and healed faultily. Hidden rifts began to distort the sphere, ballooning out one of the alcoves like a bubble of over-extended gum.

Stamers tapped my elbow.

'Lively responses, aren't they, Mr Talbot?' He put his hand on the wall behind us. The plastex swam and whirled like boiling toothpaste, then extruded itself into a small ledge.

Stamers sat down on the lip, which quickly expanded to match the contours of his body, providing back and arm rests. 'Sit down and relax, Mr Talbot, let yourself feel at home here.'

The seat cushioned up around me like an enormous white hand, and immediately the walls and ceiling quietened – obviously Stamers's first job was to get his clients off their feet before their restless shuffling could do any damage. Someone living there must have put in a lot of anguished pacing and knuckle-cracking.

'Of course, you're getting nothing but custom-built units here,' Stamers said. 'The vinyl chains in this plastex were handcrafted literally molecule by molecule.'

I felt the room shift around me. The ceiling was dilating and contracting in steady pulses, an absurdly exaggerated response to our own respiratory rhythms, but the motions were overlayed by sharp transverse spasms, feed-back from some cardiac ailment.

The house was not only frightened of us, it was seriously ill. Somebody, Dmitri Shochmann perhaps, overflowing with self-hate, had committed an appalling injury to himself, and the house was recapitulating its previous response. I was about to ask Stamers if the suicide party had been staged here when he sat up and looked around fretfully.

At the same time my ears started to sing. Mysteriously, the air pressure inside the lounge was building up, gusts of old grit whirling out into the hallway towards the exit.

Stamers was on his feet, the seat telescoping back into the wall.

'Er, Mr Talbot, let's stroll around the garden, give you the feel of –'

He broke off, face creased in alarm. The ceiling was only five feet above our heads, contracting like a huge white bladder.

'– explosive decompression,' Stamers finished automatically, taking my arm. 'I don't understand this,' he muttered as we ran out into the hallway, the air whooshing past us.

I had a shrewd idea what was happening, and sure enough we found Fay peering into the control console, swinging the volume tabs.

Stamers dived past her. We were almost dragged back into the lounge as the ceiling began its outward leg and sucked the air in through the doorway. He reached the emergency panel and switched the house off.

Wide-eyed, he buttoned his shirt. 'That was close, Mrs Talbot, really close.' He gave a light hysterical laugh.

As we walked back to the car, the giant spheres resting among the weeds, he said: 'Well, Mr Talbot, it's a fine property. A remarkable pedigree for a house only eight years old. An exciting challenge, you know, a new dimension in living.'

I gave him a weak smile. 'Maybe, but it's not exactly *us*, is it?'

We had come to Vermilion Sands for two years, while I opened a law office in downtown Red Beach twenty miles away. Apart from the dust, smog and inflationary prices of real estate in Red Beach, a strong motive for coming out to Vermilion Sands was that any number of potential clients were mouldering away there in the old mansions – forgotten movie queens, lonely impresarios and the like, some of the most litigious people in the world. Once installed, I could make my rounds of the bridge tables and dinner parties, tactfully stimulating a little righteous will-paring and contract-breaking.

However, as we drove down Stellavista on our inspection tour I wondered if we'd find anywhere suitable. Rapidly we went through a mock Assyrian ziggurat (the last owner had suffered from St Vitus's Dance, and the whole structure still jittered like a galvanized Tower of Pisa), and a converted submarine pen (here the problem had been alcoholism, we could *feel* the gloom and helplessness come down off those huge damp walls).

Finally Stamers gave up and brought us back to earth. Unfortunately his more conventional properties were little better. The real trouble was that most of Vermilion Sands is composed of early, or primitive-fantastic psychotropic, when the possibilities offered by the new bio-plastic medium rather went to architects' heads. It was some years before a compromise was reached between the one hundred per cent responsive structive and the rigid non-responsive houses of the past. The first PT houses had so many senso-cells distributed over them, echoing every shift of mood and position of the occupants, that living in one was like inhabiting someone else's brain.

Unluckily bioplastics need a lot of exercise or they grow rigid and crack, and many people believe that PT buildings are still given unnecessarily subtle memories and are far too sensitive – there's the apocryphal story of the millionaire of plebian origins who was literally frozen out of a million-dollar mansion he had bought from an aristocratic family. The place had been trained to respond to their habitual rudeness and bad temper, and reacted discordantly when readjusting itself to the millionaire, unintentionally parodying his soft-spoken politeness.

But although the echoes of previous tenants can be intrusive, this naturally has its advantages. Many medium-priced PT homes resonate with the bygone laughter of happy families, the relaxed harmony of a successful marriage. It was something like this that I wanted for Fay and myself. In the previous year our relationship had begun to fade a little, and a really well-integrated house with a healthy set of reflexes – say, those of a prosperous bank president and his devoted spouse – would go a long way towards healing the rifts between us.

Leafing through the brochures when we reached the end of Stellavista I could see that domesticated bank presidents had been in short supply at Vermilion Sands. The pedigrees were either packed with ulcer-ridden, quadri-divorced TV executives, or discreetly blank.

99 Stellavista was in the latter category. As we climbed out of the car and walked up the short drive I searched the pedigree for data on the past tenants, but only the original owner was given: a Miss Emma Slack, psychic orientation unstated.

That it was a woman's house was obvious. Shaped like an enormous orchid, it was set back on a low concrete dais in the centre of a blue gravel court. The white plastex wings, which carried the lounge on one side and the master bedroom on the other, spanned out across the magnolias on the far side of the drive. Between the two wings, on the first floor, was an open terrace around a heart-shaped swimming-pool. The terrace ran back to the central bulb, a three-storey segment containing the chauffeur's apartment and a vast two-decker kitchen.

The house seemed to be in good condition. The plastex was unscarred, its thin seams running smoothly to the far rim like the veins of a giant leaf.

Curiously, Stamers was in no hurry to switch on. He pointed to left and right as we made our way up the glass staircase to the terrace, underlining various attractive features, but made no effort to find the control console, and I suspected that the house might be a static conversion – a fair number of PT houses are frozen in one or other position at the end of their working lives, and make tolerable static homes.

'It's not bad,' I admitted, looking across the powder-blue water as Stamers piled on the superlatives. Through the glass bottom of the pool the car parked below loomed like a coloured whale asleep on the ocean bed. 'This is the sort of thing, all right. But what about switching it on?'

Stamers stepped around me and headed after Fay. 'You'll

want to see the kitchen first, Mr Talbot. There's no hurry, let yourself feel at home here.'

The kitchen was fabulous, banks of gleaming control panels and auto units. Everything was recessed and stylized, blending into the over-all colour scheme, complex gadgets folding back into self-sealing cabinets. Boiling an egg there would have taken me a couple of days.

'Quite a plant,' I commented. Fay wandered around in a daze of delight, automatically fingering the chrome. 'Looks as if it's tooled up to produce penicillin.' I tapped the brochure. 'But why so cheap? At twenty-five thousand it's damn nearly being given away.'

Stamers's eyes brightened. He flashed me a broad conspiratorial smile which indicated that this was *my* year, *my* day. Taking me off on a tour of the rumpus room and library, he began to hammer home the merits of the house, extolling his company's thirty-five year, easy-purchase plan (they wanted anything except cash – there was no money in that) and the beauty and simplicity of the garden (mostly flexible polyurethane perennials).

Finally, apparently convinced that I was sold, he switched the house on.

I didn't know then what it was, but something strange had taken place in that house. Emma Slack had certainly been a woman with a powerful and oblique personality. As I walked slowly around the empty lounge, feeling the walls angle and edge away, doorways widen when I approached, curious echoes stirred through the memories embedded in the house. The responses were undefined, but somehow eerie and unsettling, like being continually watched over one's shoulder, each room adjusting itself to my soft, random footsteps as if they contained the possibility of some explosive burst of passion or temperament.

Inclining my head, I seemed to hear other echoes, delicate and feminine, a graceful swirl of movement reflected in a brief, fluid sweep in one corner, the decorous unfolding of an archway or recess.

Then, abruptly, the mood would invert, and the hollow eeriness return.

Fay touched my arm. 'Howard, it's strange.'

I shrugged. 'Interesting, though. Remember, our own responses will overlay these within a few days.'

Fay shook her head. 'I couldn't stand it, Howard. Mr Stamers must have something normal.'

'Darling, Vermilion Sands is Vermilion Sands. Don't expect to find the suburban norms. People here were individualists.'

I looked down at Fay. Her small oval face, with its childlike mouth and chin, the fringe of blonde hair and pert nose, seemed lost and anxious.

I put my arm around her shoulder. 'O.K., sweetie, you're quite right. Let's find somewhere we can put our feet up and relax. Now, what are we going to say to Stamers?'

Surprisingly, Stamers didn't seem all that disappointed. When I shook my head he put up a token protest but soon gave in and switched off the house.

'I know how Mrs Talbot feels,' he conceded as we went down the staircase. 'Some of these places have got too much personality built into them. Living with someone like Gloria Tremayne isn't too easy.'

I stopped, two steps from the bottom, a curious ripple of recognition running through my mind.

'Gloria Tremayne? I thought the only owner was a Miss Emma Slack.'

Stamers nodded. 'Yes. Gloria Tremayne. Emma Slack was her real name. Don't say I told you, though everybody living around here knows it. We keep it quiet as long as we can. If we said Gloria Tremayne no one would even look at the place.'

'Gloria Tremayne,' Fay repeated, puzzled. 'She was the movie star who shot her husband, wasn't she? He was a famous architect – Howard, weren't you on that case?'

As Fay's voice chattered on I turned and looked up the staircase towards the sun-lounge, my mind casting itself back ten years to one of the most famous trials of the decade, whose course and verdict were as much as anything else to mark the end of a whole generation, and show up the irresponsibilities of the world before the Recess. Even though Gloria Tremayne had been acquitted, everyone knew that she had cold-bloodedly murdered her husband, the architect Miles Vanden Starr. Only the silver-tongued pleading of Daniel Hammett, her defence attorney, assisted by a young man called Howard Talbot, had saved her. I said to Fay, 'Yes, I helped to defend her. It seems a long time ago. Angel, wait in the car. I want to check something.'

Before she could follow me I ran up the staircase on to the terrace and closed the glass double doors behind me. Inert and unresponsive now, the white walls rose into the sky on either side of the pool. The water was motionless, a transparent block of condensed time, through which I could see the drowned images of Fay and Stamers sitting in the car, like an embalmed fragment of my future.

For three weeks, during her trial ten years earlier, I sat only a few feet from Gloria Tremayne, and like everyone else in that crowded courtroom I would never forget her mask-like face, the composed eyes that examined each of the witnesses as they gave their testimony – chauffeur, police surgeon, neighbours who heard the shots – like a brilliant spider arraigned by its victims, never once showing any emotion or response. As they dismembered her web, skein by skein, she sat impassively at its centre, giving Hammett no encouragement, content to repose in the image of herself ('The Ice Face') projected across the globe for the previous fifteen years.

Perhaps in the end this saved her. The jury were unable to outstare the enigma. To be honest, by the last week of the trial I had lost all interest in it. As I steered Hammett through his brief, opening and shutting his red wooden suitcase (the Hammett hallmark, it was an excellent jury distractor) whenever he indicated, my attention was fixed completely on Gloria Tremayne, trying to find some flaw in the mask through which I could glimpse her personality. I suppose that I was just another naive young man who had fallen in love with a myth manufactured by a thousand publicity agents, but for me the sensation was the real thing, and when she was acquitted the world began to revolve again.

That justice had been flouted mattered nothing. Hammett, curiously, believed her innocent. Like many successful lawyers he had based his career on the principle of prosecuting the guilty and defending the innocent – this way he was sure of a sufficiently high proportion of successes to give him a reputation for being brilliant and unbeatable. When he defended Gloria Tremayne most lawyers thought he had been tempted to depart from principle by a fat bribe from her studio, but in fact he volunteered to take the case. Perhaps he, too, was working off a secret infatuation.

Of course, I never saw her again. As soon as her next picture had been safely released her studio dropped her. Later she briefly reappeared on a narcotics charge after a car smash, and then disappeared into a limbo of alcoholics hospitals and psychiatric wards. When she died five years afterwards few newspapers gave her more than a couple of lines.

Below, Stamers sounded the horn. Leisurely I retraced my way through the lounge and bedrooms, scanning the empty floors, running my hands over the smooth plastex walls, bracing myself to feel again the impact of Gloria Tremayne's personality.

Blissfully, her presence would be everywhere in the house, a thousand echoes of her distilled into every matrix and senso-cell, each moment of emotion blended into a replica more intimate than anyone, apart from her dead husband, could ever know. The Gloria Tremayne with whom I had become infatuated had ceased to exist, but this house was the shrine that entombed the very signatures of her soul.

To begin with everything went quietly. Fay remonstrated with me, but I promised her a new mink wrap out of the savings we made on the house. Secondly, I was careful to keep the volume down for the first few weeks, so that there would be no clash of feminine wills. A major problem of psychotropic houses is that after several months one has to increase the volume to get the same image of the last owner, and this increases the sensitivity of the memory cells and their rate of contamination. At the same time, magnifying the psychic underlay emphasizes the cruder emotional ground-base. One begins to taste the lees rather than the distilled cream of the previous tenancy. I wanted to savour the quintessence of Gloria Tremayne as long as possible so I deliberately rationed myself, turning the volume down during the day while I was out, then switching on only those rooms in which I sat in the evenings.

Right from the outset I was neglecting Fay. Not only were we both preoccupied with the usual problems of adjustment faced by every married couple moving into a new house – undressing in the master bedroom that first night was a positive honeymoon debut all over again – but I was completely immersed in the exhilarating persona of Gloria Tremayne, exploring every alcove and niche in search of her.

In the evenings I sat in the library, feeling her around me in the stirring walls, hovering nearby as I emptied the packing cases like an attendant succubus. Sipping my Scotch while night closed over the dark blue pool, I carefully analysed her personality, deliberately varying my moods to evoke as wide a range of responses. The memory cells in the house were perfectly bonded, never revealing any flaws of character, always reposed and self-controlled. If I leapt out of my chair and switched the stereogram abruptly from Stravinsky to Stan Kenton to the MJQ, the room adjusted its mood and tempo without effort.

And yet how long was it before I discovered that there was another personality present in that house, and began to feel the curious eeriness Fay and I had noticed as soon as Stamers switched the house on? Not for a few weeks, when the house was still responding to my star-struck idealism. While my devotion to the departed spirit of Gloria Tremayne was the dominant mood, the house played itself back accordingly, recapitulating only the more serene aspects of Gloria Tremayne's character.

Soon, however, the mirror was to darken.

It was Fay who broke the spell. She quickly realized that the initial responses were being overlayed by others from a more mellow and, from her point of view, more dangerous quarter of the past. After doing her best to put up with them she made a few guarded attempts to freeze Gloria out, switching the volume controls up and down, selecting the maximum of bass lift – which stressed the masculine responses – and the minimum of alto lift.

One morning I caught her on her knees by the console, poking a screwdriver at the memory drum, apparently in an effort to erase the entire store.

Taking it from her, I locked the unit and hooked the key on to my chain.

'Darling, the mortgage company could sue us for destroying the pedigree. Without it this house would be valueless. What are you trying to do?'

Fay dusted her hands on her skirt and stared me straight in the eye, chin jutting.

'I'm trying to restore a little sanity here and if possible, find my own marriage again. I thought it might be in there somewhere.'

I put my arm around her and steered her back towards the kitchen. 'Darling, you're getting over-intuitive again. Just relax, don't try to upset everything.'

'Upset –? Howard, what are you talking about? Haven't I a right to my own husband? I'm sick of sharing him with a homicidal neurotic who died five years ago. It's positively ghoulish!'

I winced as she snapped this out, feeling the walls in the hallway darken and retreat defensively. The air became clouded and frenetic, like a dull storm-filled day.

'Fay, you know your talent for exaggeration...' I searched around for the kitchen, momentarily disoriented as the corridor walls shifted and backed. 'You don't know how lucky you –'

I didn't get any further before she interrupted. Within five seconds we were in the middle of a blistering row. Fay threw all caution to the winds, deliberately, I think, in the hope of damaging the house permanently, while I stupidly let a lot of my unconscious resentment towards her come out. Finally she stormed away into her bedroom and I stamped into the shattered lounge and slumped down angrily on the sofa.

Above me the ceiling flexed and quivered, the colour of roof slates, here and there mottled by angry veins that bunched the walls in on each other. The air pressure mounted but I felt too tired to open a window and sat stewing in a pit of black anger.

It must have been then that I recognized the presence of Miles Vanden Starr. All echoes of Gloria Tremayne's personality had vanished, and for the first time since moving in I had recovered my normal perspectives. The mood of anger and resentment in the lounge was remarkably persistent, far longer than expected from what had been little more than a tiff. The walls continued to pulse and knot for over half an hour, long after my own irritation had faded and I was sitting up and examining the room clear-headedly.

The anger, deep and frustrated, was obviously masculine. I assumed, correctly, that the original source had been Vanden Starr, who had designed the house for Gloria Tremayne and lived there for over a year before his death. To have so grooved the memory drum meant that this atmosphere of blind, neurotic hostility had been maintained for most of that time.

As the resentment slowly dispersed I could see that for the time being Fay had succeeded in her object. The serene persona of Gloria Tremayne had vanished. The feminine motif was still there, in a higher and shriller key, but the dominant presence was distinctly Vanden Starr's. This new mood of the house reminded me of the courtroom photographs of him; glowering out of 1950-ish groups with Le Corbusier and Lloyd Wright, stalking about some housing project in Chicago or Tokyo like a petty dictator, heavy-jowled, thyroidal, with large lustreless eyes, and then the Vermilion Sands: 1970 shots of him, fitting into the movie colony like a shark into a goldfish bowl.

However, there was power behind those baleful drives. Cued in by our tantrum, the presence of Vanden Starr had descended upon 99 Stellavista like a thundercloud. At first I tried to recapture the earlier halcyon mood, but this had disappeared and my irritation at losing it only served to inflate the thundercloud. An unfortunate aspect of psychotropic houses is the factor of resonance – diametrically opposed personalities soon stabilize their relationship, the echo inevitably yielding to the new source. But where the personalities are of similar frequency and amplitude they mutually reinforce themselves, each adapting itself for comfort to the personality of the other. All too soon I began to assume the character of

Vanden Starr, and my increased exasperation with Fay merely drew from the house a harder front of antagonism.

Later I knew that I was, in fact, treating Fay in exactly the way that Vanden Starr had treated Gloria Tremayne, recapitulating the steps of their tragedy with consequences that were equally disastrous.

Fay recognized the changed mood of the house immediately. 'What's happened to our lodger?' she gibed at dinner the next evening. 'Our beautiful ghost seems to be spurning you. Is the spirit unwilling although the flesh is weak?'

'God knows,' I growled testily. 'I think you've really messed the place up.' I glanced around the dining room for any echo of Gloria Tremayne, but she had gone. Fay went out to the kitchen and I sat over my half-eaten hors d'oeuvres, staring at it blankly, when I felt a curious ripple in the wall behind me, a silver dart of movement that vanished as soon as I looked up. I tried to focus it without success, the first echo of Gloria since our row, but later that evening, when I went into Fay's bedroom after I heard her crying, I noticed it again.

Fay had gone into the bathroom. As I was about to find her I felt the same echo of feminine anguish. It had been prompted by Fay's tears, but like Vanden Starr's mood set off by my own anger, it persisted long after the original cue. I followed it into the corridor as it faded out of the room but it diffused outwards into the ceiling and hung there motionlessly.

Starting to walk down to the lounge, I realized that the house was watching me like a wounded animal.

Two days later came the attack on Fay.

I had just returned home from the office, childishly annoyed with Fay for parking her car on my side of the garage. In the cloakroom I tried to check my anger; the senso-cells had picked up the cue and began to suck the irritation out of me, pouring it back into the air until the walls of the cloakroom darkened and seethed.

I shouted some gratuitous insult at Fay, who was in the lounge. A second later she screamed: 'Howard! Quickly!'

Running towards the lounge, I flung myself at the door, expecting it to retract. Instead, it remained rigid, frame locked in the archway. The entire house seemed grey and strained, the pool outside like a tank of cold lead.

Fay shouted again. I seized the metal handle of the manual control and wrenched the door back.

Fay was almost out of sight, on one of the slab sofas in the centre of the room, buried beneath the sagging canopy of the ceiling which had collapsed on to her. The heavy plastex had flowed together directly above her head, forming a blob a yard in diameter.

Raising the flaccid plastex with my hands, I managed to lift it off Fay, who was spread-eagled into the cushions with only her feet protruding. She wriggled out and flung her arms around me, sobbing noiselessly.

'Howard, this house is insane, I think it's trying to kill me!'

'For heaven's sake, Fay, don't be silly. It was simply a freak accumulation of senso-cells. Your breathing probably set it off.' I patted her shoulder, remembering the child I had married a few years earlier. Smiling to myself, I watched the ceiling retract slowly, the walls grow lighter in tone.

'Howard, can't we leave here?' Fay babbled. 'Let's go and live in a static house. I know it's dull, but what does it matter–?'

'Well,' I said, 'it's not just dull, it's dead. Don't worry, angel, you'll learn to like it here.'

Fay twisted away from me. 'Howard, I can't stay in this house any more. You've been so preoccupied recently, you're completely changed.' She started to cry again, and pointed at the ceiling. 'If I hadn't been lying down, do you realize it would have killed me?'

I dusted the end of the sofa. 'Yes, I can see your heel marks.' Irritation welled up like bile before I could stop it. 'I thought I told you not to stretch out here. This isn't a beach, Fay. You know it annoys me.'

Around us the walls began to mottle and cloud again.

Why did Fay anger me so easily? Was it, as I assumed at the time, unconscious resentment that egged me on, or was I merely a vehicle for the antagonism which had accumulated during Vanden Starr's marriage to Gloria Tremayne and was now venting itself on the hapless couple who followed them to 99 Stellavista? Perhaps I'm over-charitable to myself in assuming the latter, but Fay and I had been tolerably happy during our five years of marriage, and I am sure my nostalgic infatuation for Gloria Tremayne couldn't have so swept me off my feet.

Either way, however, Fay didn't wait for a second attempt. Two days later I came home to find a fresh tape on the kitchen memophone. I switched it on to hear her tell me that she could no longer put up with me, my nagging or 99 Stellavista and was going back east to stay with her sister.

Callously, my first reaction, after the initial twinge of indignation, was sheer relief. I still believed that Fay was responsible for Gloria Tremayne's eclipse and the emergence of Vanden Starr, and that with her gone I would recapture the early days of idyll and romance.

I was only partly right. Gloria Tremayne did return, but not in the role expected. I, who had helped to defend her at her trial, should have known better.

A few days after Fay left I became aware that the house had taken on a separate existence, its coded memories discharging themselves independently of my own behaviour. Often when I returned in the evening, eager to relax over half a decanter of Scotch, I would find the ghosts of Miles Vanden Starr and

Gloria Tremayne in full flight. Starr's black and menacing personality crowded after the tenuous but increasingly resilient quintessence of his wife. This rapier-like resistance could be observed literally – the walls of the lounge would stiffen and darken in a vortex of anger that converged upon a small zone of lightness hiding in one of the alcoves, as if to obliterate its presence, but at the last moment Gloria's persona would flit nimbly away, leaving the room to seethe and writhe.

Fay had set off this spirit of resistance, and I visualized Gloria Tremayne going through a similar period of living hell. As her personality re-emerged in its new role I watched it carefully, volume at maximum despite the damage the house might do to itself. Once Stamers stopped by and offered to get the circuits checked for me. He had seen the house from the road, flexing and changing colour like an anguished squid. Thanking him, I made up some excuse and declined. Later he told me that I had kicked him out unceremoniously – apparently he hardly recognized me; I was striding around the dark quaking house like a madman in an Elizabethan horror tragedy, oblivious of everything.

Although submerged by the personality of Miles Vanden Starr, I gradually realized that Gloria Tremayne had been deliberately driven out of her mind by him. What had prompted his implacable hostility I can only hazard – perhaps he resented her success, perhaps she had been unfaithful to him. When she finally retaliated and shot him it was, I'm sure, an act of self-defence.

Two months after she went east Fay filed a divorce suit against me. Frantically I telephoned her, explaining that I would be grateful if she postponed the action as the publicity would probably kill my new law office. However, Fay was adamant. What annoyed me most was that she sounded better than she had done for years, really happy again. When I pleaded with her she said she needed the divorce in order to marry again, and then, as a last straw, refused to tell me who the man was.

By the time I slammed the phone down my temper was taking off like a lunar probe. I left the office early and began a tour of the bars in Red Beach, working my way slowly back to Vermilion Sands. I hit 99 Stellavista like a one-man task force, mowing down most of the magnolias in the drive, ramming the car into the garage on the third pass after wrecking both auto-doors.

My keys jammed in the door lock and I finally had to kick my way through one of the glass panels. Raging upstairs on to the darkened terrace I flung my hat and coat into the pool and slammed into the lounge. By 2 a.m., as I mixed myself a night-cap at the bar and put the last act of *Götterdämmerung* on the stereogram, the whole place was really warming up.

On the way to bed I lurched into Fay's room to see what damage I could do to the memories I still retained of her, kicked in a wardrobe and booted the mattress on to the floor, turning the walls literally blue with a salvo of epithets.

Shortly after three o'clock I fell asleep, the house revolving around me like an enormous turntable.

It must have been only four o'clock when I woke, conscious of a curious silence in the darkened room. I was stretched across the bed, one hand around the neck of the decanter, the other holding a dead cigar stub. The walls were motionless, unstirred by even the residual eddies which drift through a psychotropic house when the occupants are asleep.

Something had altered the normal perspectives of the room. Trying to focus on the grey underswell of the ceiling, I listened for footsteps outside. Sure enough, the corridor wall began to retract. The archway, usually a six-inch wide slit, rose to admit someone. Nothing came through, but the room expanded to accommodate an additional presence, the ceiling ballooning upwards. Astounded, I tried not to move my head, watching the unoccupied pressure zone move quickly across the room towards the bed, its motion shadowed by a small dome in the ceiling.

The pressure zone paused at the foot of the bed and hesitated for a few seconds. But instead of stabilizing, the walls began to vibrate rapidly, quivering with strange uncertain tremors, radiating a sensation of acute urgency and indecision.

Then, abruptly, the room stilled. A second later, as I lifted myself up on one elbow, a violent spasm convulsed the room, buckling the walls and lifting the bed off the floor. The entire house started to shake and writhe. Gripped by this seizure, the bedroom contracted and expanded like the chamber of a dying heart, the ceiling rising and falling.

I steadied myself on the swinging bed and gradually the convulsion died away, the walls realigning. I stood up, wondering what insane crisis this psychotropic *grande mal* duplicated.

The room was in darkness, thin moonlight coming through the trio of small circular vents behind the bed. These were contracting as the walls closed in on each other. Pressing my hands against the ceiling, I felt it push downwards strongly. The edges of the floor were blending into the walls as the room converted itself into a sphere.

The air pressure mounted. I tumbled over to the vents, reached them as they clamped around my fists, air whistling through my fingers. Face against the openings, I gulped in the cool night air, and tried to force apart the locking plastex.

The safety cut-out switch was above the door on the other side of the room. I dived across to it, clambering over the tilting bed, but the flowing plastex had submerged the whole unit.

Head bent to avoid the ceiling, I pulled off my tie, gasping at the thudding air. Trapped in the room, I was suffocating as it duplicated the expiring breaths of Vanden Starr after he had been shot. The tremendous spasm had been his convulsive reaction as the bullet from Gloria Tremayne's gun crashed into his chest.

I fumbled in my pockets for a knife, felt my cigarette lighter, pulled it out and flicked it on. The room was now a grey sphere ten feet in diameter. Thick veins, as broad as my arm, were knotting across its surface, crushing the endboards of the bedstead.

I raised the lighter to the surface of the ceiling, and let it play across the opaque fluoglass. Immediately it began to fizz and bubble. It flared alight and split apart, the two burning lips unzipping in a brilliant discharge of heat.

As the cocoon bisected itself, I could see the twisted mouth of the corridor bending into the room below the sagging outline of the dining room ceiling. Feet skating in the molten plastex, I pulled myself up on to the corridor. The whole house seemed to have been ruptured. Walls were buckled. floors furling at their edges. Water was pouring out of the pool as the unit tipped forwards on the weakened foundations. The glass slabs of the staircase had been shattered, the razor-like teeth jutting from the wall.

I ran into Fay's bedroom, found the cut-out switch and stabbed the sprinkler alarm.

The house was still throbbing, but a moment later it locked and became rigid. I leaned against the dented wall and let the spray pour across my face from the sprinkler jets.

Around me, its wings torn and disarrayed, the house reared up like a tortured flower.

Standing in the trampled flower beds, Stamers gazed at the house, an expression of awe and bewilderment on his face. It was just after six o'clock. The last of the three police cars had driven away, the lieutenant in charge finally conceding defeat. 'Dammit, I can't arrest a house for attempted homicide, can I?' he'd asked me somewhat belligerently. I roared with laughter at this, my initial feelings of shock having given way to an almost hysterical sense of fun.

Stamers found me equally difficult to understand.

'What on earth were you doing in there?' he asked, voice down to a whisper.

'Nothing. I tell you I was fast asleep. And relax. The house can't hear you. It's switched off.'

We wandered across the churned gravel and waded through the water which lay like a black mirror. Stamers shook his head.

'The place must have been insane. If you ask me it needs a psychiatrist to straighten it out.'

'You're right,' I told him. 'In fact, that was exactly my role – to reconstruct the original traumatic situation and release the repressed material.'

'Why joke about it? It tried to kill you.'

'Don't be absurd. The real culprit is Vanden Starr. But as the lieutenant implied, you can't arrest a man who's been dead for ten years. It was the pent-up memory of his death which tried to kill me. Even if Gloria Tremayne was driven to pulling the trigger, Starr pointed the gun. Believe me, I lived out his role for a couple of months. What worries me is that if Fay hadn't had enough good sense to leave she might have been hypnotized by the persona of Gloria Tremayne into killing *me*.'

Much to Stamers's surprise, I decided to stay on at 99 Stellavista. Apart from the fact that I hadn't enough cash to buy another place, the house had certain undeniable memories for me that I didn't want to forsake. Gloria Tremayne was still there, and I was sure that Vanden Starr had at last gone. The kitchen and service units were still functional, and apart from their contorted shapes most of the rooms were habitable. In addition I needed a rest, and nothing is so quiet as a static house.

Of course, in its present form 99 Stellavista can hardly be

regarded as a typical static dwelling. Yet, the deformed rooms and twisted corridors have as much personality as any psychotropic house. The PT unit is still working and one day I shall switch it on again. But one thing worries me. The violent spasms which ruptured the house may in some way have damaged Gloria Tremayne's personality. To live with it might well be madness for me, as there's a subtle charm about the house even in its distorted form, like the ambiguous smile of a beautiful but insane woman.

Often I unlock the control console and examine the memory drum. Her personality, whatever it may be, is there. Nothing would be simpler than to erase it. But I can't.

One day soon, whatever the outcome, I know that I shall have to switch the house on again.

## THE HISTORY OF VINTAGE

The famous American publisher Alfred A. Knopf (1892–1984) founded Vintage Books in the United States in 1954 as a paperback home for the authors published by his company. Vintage was launched in the United Kingdom in 1990 and works independently from the American imprint although both are part of the international publishing group, Random House.

Vintage in the United Kingdom was initially created to publish paperback editions of books bought by the prestigious literary hardback imprints in the Random House Group such as Jonathan Cape, Chatto & Windus, Hutchinson and later William Heinemann, Secker & Warburg and The Harvill Press. There are many Booker and Nobel Prize-winning authors on the Vintage list and the imprint publishes a huge variety of fiction and non-fiction. Over the years Vintage has expanded and the list now includes great authors of the past – who are published under the Vintage Classics imprint – as well as many of the most influential authors of the present. In 2012 Vintage Children's Classics was launched to include the much-loved authors of our youth.

www.vintage-classics.info

Visit www.worldofstories.co.uk for all your favourite children's classics